BUDDHIST TALES for YOUNG and OLD

Volume 3

Stories of the Enlightenment Being

Jātakas 101–150

Interpreted by

KURUNEGODA PIYATISSA MAHA THERA

Stories Retold by

STEPHAN HILLYER LEVITT

Pariyatti Press

Buddhist Tales for Young and Old

Volume 1: STORIES OF THE ENLIGHTENMENT BEING, Jātakas 1–50.
Interpreted by Kurunegoda Piyatissa Maha Thera. Stories Told by Todd Anderson. Illustrated by Sally Bienemann, Millie Byrum, Mark Gilson. 2nd edition, revised and enlarged by Kurunegoda Piyatissa Maha Thera and Stephan Hillyer Levitt. Parkside Hills, New York: Buddhist Literature Society, Inc., 2013. (1st edition, under the title PRINCE GOODSPEAKER, STORIES 1–50, 1995.)

Volume 2: STORIES OF THE ENLIGHTENMENT BEING, Jātakas 51–100, 514.
Interpreted by Kurunegoda Piyatissa Maha Thera. Stories Told by Todd Anderson. Illustrated by John Patterson. 2nd edition, revised and enlarged by Kurunegoda Piyatissa Maha Thera and Stephan Hillyer Levitt. Parkside Hills, New York: Buddhist Literature Society, Inc., 2013. (1st edition, under the title KING FRUITFUL, STORIES 51–100, 1996. 2nd ptg. of the 1st edition, together with KING SIX TUSKER AND THE QUEEN WHO HATED HIM, CHADDANTA-JATAKA (NO. 514) appended, [2004].)

Volume 3: STORIES OF THE ENLIGHTENMENT BEING, Jātakas 101–150.
Interpreted by Kurunegoda Piyatissa Maha Thera. Stories Retold by Stephan Hillyer Levitt. Parkside Hills, New York: Buddhist Literature Society, Inc., 2007.

Volume 4: STORIES OF THE ENLIGHTENMENT BEING, Jātakas 151–200.
Interpreted by Kurunegoda Piyatissa Maha Thera. Stories Retold by Stephan Hillyer Levitt. Parkside Hills, New York: Buddhist Literature Society, Inc., 2009.

Volume 5: STORIES OF THE ENLIGHTENMENT BEING, Jātakas 201–250.
Interpreted by Kurunegoda Piyatissa Maha Thera. Stories Retold by Stephan Hillyer Levitt. Parkside Hills, New York: Buddhist Literature Society, Inc., 2012.

BUDDHIST TALES for YOUNG and OLD

Volume 3

Stories of the Enlightenment Being

Jātakas 101–150

Remains of the Buddha's Living Chamber in
Jetavanārāma in Sāvatthi

Pariyatti Press
an imprint of
Pariyatti Publishing
www.pariyatti.org

First Pariyatti Edition, 2024
Published with the consent of Buddhist Literature Society, Inc.

ISBN: 978-1-68172-659-5 (Print)
ISBN: 978-1-68172-681-6 (PDF)
ISBN: 978-1-68172-682-3 (ePub)
ISBN: 978-1-68172-683-0 (Mobi)
Library of Congress Control Number: 2024936371

Cover illustration by Sally Bienemann, assisted by Arlene Yellen and cover design by Nalin Ariyarathne.

Foreword

Due to unexpected circumstances, it was necessary to postpone the translation of the Jātaka stories that had been begun in Volumes 1 and 2. My co-author had to leave the work on account of his getting married. And I was very much occupied at my temple as it was undertaking the construction of a new building. It took eight years to complete this work.

I thank the Buddha Educational Foundation for its understanding patience while waiting for Volume 3.

My new co-author, Dr. Stephan Levitt, who is a very skilled writer, has undertaken to help me with the preparation of this volume. He has not only retold my interpretation of the stories, but he is also responsible for the word processing of the text on his own personal computer, for proofreading the manuscript, for making an audio version of the text for CD distribution, and he will as well proofread the printer's proofs.

It is good news that even before Volume 3 is sent to the printer, Volumes 1 and 2 have been reprinted twice. Thanks must go to the Buddha Educational Foundation for its dedication and its invaluable Dhamma-Dāna, its invaluable Gift of Dhamma. I am encouraged greatly by its efforts.

According to the *Mahāvaṃsa*, the Great Chronicle of Sri Lanka, the most Venerable Arahant Mahā Mahinda introduced Buddhism to the ancient Sri Lankan community by preaching the Buddhist stories of the *Petavatthu*, the *Vimānavatthu*, and the *Jātaka*.

Sri Lankans are known as a people who enrich their minds through Jātaka stories. Even today in remote village temples of Sri Lanka there are three months of preaching every year. This is to educate the villagers. During this period, village children learn by listening to the stories coming from the *Jātaka*.

Buddhist culture and civilization developed by following the examples of good human qualities that are espoused in the Jātaka stories. Sri Lankan Buddhists learn to follow these Buddhist values from their religious teachers from the time they are young.

Sri Lanka is a very small country that can scarcely be seen on a world map, with only a small population. Yet, over 2200 years ago a 332-foot high Stūpa was built in Sri Lanka that is still in good condition. Ordinary people in the country built this Stūpa in only a few years during the reign of the great king Duṭṭhagāmaṇi. Imagine! Ordinary Sri Lankans built such a solid building with man-made bricks during the time of this ruler by hand, using very undeveloped tools. And it still exists today! While unbelievable, this is true. The building is in excellent condition. Thousands of tourists visit daily to see this miraculous building.

How did ancient Sri Lankans gain such craftsmanship and technical knowledge, and such architectural expertise? They gained such abilities through Buddhist practical knowledge. During the time of the same king, they also built a nine-story building. Even today, there remain from this 1600 carved stone pillars. It was the tallest building ever heard of in its time. This was recorded in the *Mahāvaṃsa*, the Great Chronicle, and in other histories written in Pāli and in Sinhala by Buddhist monks.

If one studies the history of the Sri Lankan island, one can come across many such results of the learning taught in Jātaka stories and other such texts. There are many such things reported in Sri Lankan Pāli and Sinhala literature.

Unfortunately, most of Sri Lanka's ancient literature was burnt and destroyed by South Indian invaders and the Portuguese, as well as by other Western invaders. The background of the few remaining books mostly comes from Jātaka stories. Most of the extant Sri Lankan literature is based on extractions from the *Jātaka*. We have, for instance, *Kav silumiṇa, Kusa dā kava, Guttila kava, Kāvyasekharaya, Sandakinduru dā kava*, among many other of the few poetic works remaining, all of which are based on Jātaka stories.

We can see Jātaka tales illustrated in the carvings and murals of the Indian rock cut caves of Nāgārjunīkoṇḍā, Ellorā, and Ajantā. In Buddhist monasteries in Sri Lanka and elsewhere, there are countless murals based on these stories. Again in India, the railing of the famous Stūpa at Amarāvatī and the gateways at the famous Stūpa complex at Sāñcī are decorated with sculpture depicting Jātaka stories. In Java, in Indonesia, the famous Stūpa of Borobudur also has Jātaka stories depicted in reliefs on its walls and balustrades, along with the stories of other well-known Buddhist texts. Jātaka stories have as well greatly influenced Chinese and Japanese artwork. Jātaka stories are depicted, for instance, in murals in the rock cut caves at Dunhuang in Central Asia, in Western China, on the famous silk route between China and the Middle East.

Since their introduction to the Sri Lankan nation in the 3rd century B.C.E., the *Jātaka* has been promoted in Sri Lanka. Sri Lanka as a nation developed under the influence of these stories fully, until the Portuguese invaded in 1505 C.E. Even until the introduction of television to Sri Lanka, the country's people did not give up their tradition of being entertained and taught by Jātaka stories.

We must try to protect this living tradition in the modern day, and preserve the ancient Jātaka stories that are comparable, for instance, to Aesop's ancient Greek fables.

The sources used in the preparation of this translation are as follows:

1. *Jātakapāli, with the Sinhala Translation*, by Ven. Madihe Siri Paññasīha Mahā Nāyaka Thera, 3 vols. *Buddha Jayanti Tripitaka Series*, vols. 30-32. Colombo: Published under the patronage of Democratic Socialist Republican Government of Sri Lanka, 1983-86. Original Pāli Jātaka stories with the Pāli commentary, in Sinhala script with a modern Sinhala translation.
2. *Bhadantācariya Buddhaghosa Mahā Thera's Commentary to the Jātaka Pāli*, rev. and ed. by Ven. Pandit Widurupola Piyatissa Mahā Nāyaka Thera, 7 vols. *Simon Hewavitarne Bequest*, vols. 20, 24, 32, 36, 37, 39, 41. Colombo: Published by the Trustees, 1926-39. Commentary in Pāli on the Pāli Jātaka stories, based on older sources, attributed to the 5th c. C.E. scholar Buddhaghosa. An earlier edition in Sinhala script of the Pāli text in 1. above.

3. *Pansiyapaṇas Jātaka Pota*, by Virasiṃha Pratirāja. Ed. D. Jinaratana. 1927; 5th ptg. Colombo: Jinalankara Press, 1928. A late 13th – early 14th c. C.E. translation of the Pāli Jātaka stories into Sinhala by a minister of Kings Parākramabāhu II, III, and IV.
4. *Pansiyapaṇas Jātaka Pota*, by Virasiṃha Pratirāja. Ed. Vēragoḍa Amaramōli. Colombo: Ratnakara Bookshop, 1961. A different edition of 3. above.
5. *Pansiyapaṇas Jātaka Pot Vahansē*, by H. W. Nimal Prematilake. 1963; Rpt. Bandaragama: H. W. Nimal Prematilaka, 1987. Recent Sinhala summaries of the Pāli Jātaka stories.
6. *The Jātaka, or Stories of the Buddha's Former Births*, 6 vols., index. Ed. E. B. Cowell. 1895-1913; Rpt. London: Pali Text Society, 1981. English translation of the Pāli Jātaka stories done by various hands. Contains the stories of the present, which are from the commentary.

The numbers of the various Jātaka stories in this translation are as in 1. and 6. above. The sequence is also the same as in 2., but the numbering in that is different. 2. numbers the Jātaka stories according to book, chapter, and Jātaka story within a chapter.

Thanks are due to our readers, and to the Buddha Educational Foundation for their generosity.

May all attain Nibbāna!

Kurunegoda Piyatissa
October, 2005

Buddhist Literature Society, Inc.
New York Buddhist Vihara
214-22 Spencer Avenue
Parkside Hills, New York 11427-1821, U. S. A.

A Guide to the Pronunciation of Pāli Words and Names

Vowels

a	as *u* in but	u	as *u* in pull	ā	as *a* in father
ū	as *u* in rule	i	as *i* in pin	e	as *ay* in say
ī	as *i* in machine	o	as *o* in go		

Consonants and Nasals

k (guttural) like the English *k* in take or pick. kh as *kh* in lakehouse. g as *g* in pig. gh as *gh* in doghouse. The nasal ṅ is used with k, kh, g, and gh.

c (palatal) similar to *ch* in chalk, but unaspirated. ch as *ch* in chalk or church.

j like the English *g* in page. jh as *j* in joy, but even more aspirated. The nasal ñ as in Spanish Español is used with c, ch, j, and jh.

ṭ a retroflex sound, pronounced with the tongue curled back so that it touches the roof of the mouth. ṭh is the same sound, but aspirated. ḍ and ḍh are the voiced counterparts of these sounds. ṇ is the retroflex nasal. The difference between these sounds and the dentals, without dots, is not important for the general reader.

t (dental) similar to *t* in French or Italian. th as *th* in anthill. d similar to *d* in pod or paid. dh as *dh* in roundhouse. The nasal n is used with t, th, d, and dh.

p (labial) as *p* in English up. ph as *ph* in uphill. b as *b* in rub. bh as *bh* in clubhouse. The nasal m is used with p, ph, b, and bh.

ṁ as *ng* in sing. This is a nasal sound that lacks the closure of the organs required for the other nasal sounds.

Semivowels

y, r, l, v similar to their English counterparts. ḷ is a retroflex variant of l.

Sibilant

s as *s* in saint or hiss.

Aspirate

h as *h* in hit.

Contents

Foreword vii
A Guide to the Pronunciation of Pāli Words and Names xi

101 - The Story of More than a Hundred (*Parosata-Jātaka*) 1
102 - The Story of the Greengrocer (*Paṇṇika-Jātaka*) 2
103 - The Story of Hostile Action (*Veri-Jātaka*) 5
104 - The Story of Mittavindaka [One Who Enjoys His Friends] (*Mittavinda-Jātaka*) 7
105 - The Story of Weak Timber (*Dubbalakaṭṭha-Jātaka*) 9
106 - The Story of Infatuation with an Unmarried Girl of Marriageable Age (*Udañcani-Jātaka*) 11
107 - The Story of the Slinging Stone (*Sālittaka-Jātaka*) 14
108 - The Story of the Woman from Bāhiya State (*Bāhiya-Jātaka*) 18
109 - The Story of a Sweetcake of Husk Powder (*Kuṇḍakapūva-Jātaka*) 22
110 - The Dilemma Regarding All [Fragrances] Mixed (*Sabbasaṃhāraka-Pañha*) 25
111 - The Question about the Donkey (*Gadabha-Pañha*) 28
112 - The Dilemma of Princess Amarā [The Dilemma of the Hidden Road, The Dilemma of the Maiden] (*Amarādevī-Pañha, Channapatha-Pañha, Strī-Pañha*) 32
113 - The Story of the Jackal (*Sigāla-Jātaka*) 36
114 - The Story of a Proper Thinking Fish (*Mitacinti-Jātaka*) 38
115 - The Story of a Bird [The Story of a Bird That Warned Others] (*Sakuṇa-Jātaka, Anusāsika-Jātaka*) 41
116 - The Story of Disregarded Advice (*Dubacca-Jātaka*) 43
117 - The Story of the Partridge (*Tittira-Jātaka*) 45
118 - The Story of the Quail (*Vaṭṭaka-Jātaka*) 49
119 - The Story of the Rooster That Crows at the Wrong Time (*Akālarāvi-Jātaka*) 52
120 - The Story of Being Released from Bondage (*Bandhanamokkha-Jātaka*) 54
121 - The Story Regarding a Blade of Kusa Grass (*Kusanāḷi-Jātaka*) 59
122 - The Story of an Unwise Person (*Dummedha-Jātaka*) 61

123 - The Story of a Plough Handle (*Naṅgalīsa-Jātaka*) 64
124 - The Story of Water (*Amba-Jātaka*) 67
125 - The Story of Kaṭāhaka [One Who is an Empty Cauldron] (*Kaṭāhaka-Jātaka*) 69
126 - The Story of the Characteristics of Swords (*Asilakkhaṇa-Jātaka*) 73
127 - The Story of Kalaṇḍuka (*Kalaṇḍuka-Jātaka*) 76
128 - The Story of the Cat (*Biḷāra-Jātaka*) 78
129 - The Story of the Jackal That Worshipped Fire (*Aggika-Jātaka*) 81
130 - The Story of a Lazy Person (*Kosiya-Jātaka*) 83
131 - The Story of an Ill-Treated Gift (*Asampadāna-Jātaka*) 86
132 - The Story of Five Sensual Delights (*Pañcagaru-Jātaka*) 89
133 - The Story of [Sacrificial Fire] Eating (or, Being Sprinkled with) Ghee (*Ghatāsana-Jātaka*) 92
134 - The Story of Clarifying Mental Absorption [The Story of the Jewel in the Flower] (*Jhānasodhana-Jātaka, Puppharatna-Jātaka*) 94
135 - The Story of Moonbeams (*Candābha-Jātaka*) 96
136 - The Story of the Golden Swan (*Suvaṇṇahaṃsa-Jātaka*) 97
137 - The Story of the Cats (*Babbu-Jātaka*) 100
138 - The Story of an Iguana (*Godha-Jātaka*) 104
139 - The Story of One Who Had Lost in Two Ways (*Ubhatobhaṭṭha-Jātaka*) 106
140 - The Story of Crows (*Kāka-Jātaka*) 108
141 - The Story of an Iguana (*Godha-Jātaka*) 112
142 - The Story of a Jackal (*Sigāla-Jātaka*) 114
143 - The Story of Shining Forth (*Virocana-Jātaka*) 116
144 - The Story of a Tail (*Naṅguṭṭha-Jātaka*) 120
145 - The Story of Rādha (*Rādha-Jātaka*) 123
146 - The Story of a Crow (*Kāka-Jātaka*) 126
147 - The Story of Safflower (*Puppharatta-Jātaka*) 129
148 - The Story of a Jackal (*Sigāla-Jātaka*) 131
149 - The Story of One Leaf [The Story of Shining Forth] (*Ekapaṇṇa-Jātaka, Virocana-Jātaka*) 135
150 - The Story of Sañjīva (*Sañjīva-Jātaka*) 139

101

The Story of More than a Hundred
(*Parosata-Jātaka*)

This story is in all respects the same as the Parosahassa-Jātaka [No. 99], with only a few words being different.

The moral: "One should listen to wisdom when it is spoken."

102

The Story of the Greengrocer
(*Paṇṇika-Jātaka*)

At one time the Buddha who was the teacher of the three worlds and who was endowed with eighty features of beauty was living at the temple of the Jeta grove. This story was told with regard to a greengrocer.

There was a greengrocer who was a pious person with a great confidence in the value of the three jewels. He collected different spices such as ginger and turmeric, green leaves, pumpkins, and cucumbers, and sold them to make his living. He had a very beautiful daughter who was pleasing to everyone who looked at her. She was endowed with the fear and shame of doing any wrong. She always smiled. Many people of her class came to ask for her to marry them. As this girl was always smiling and pleasing others, her father doubted her purity. Therefore, her father wanted to examine her to find out whether or not she was a virgin.[1] To this end, he asked her to carry for him a box, pretending they were going to pick wild leaves. Once in the forest the father also pretended that he had lustful thoughts, and he took her hand in such a fashion as to try to persuade her to be loving.

At the moment he took her hand she began to cry and lament, and said to him, "My lord, father. This is not good for you. This is something unnatural like fire coming from water. It is not good for such an unwholesome act to be done by a person such as your lordship."

On hearing this, the father said, "Oh, my mother. I touched you that way to examine your nature. Now you can go home. I wanted to know whether or not you were a virgin." He then requested of her to let him disclose her purity.

---

1 At that time, if a girl was given in marriage and was not a virgin, her parents would be held responsible.

Thereupon she said, "My lord, father. I have my virginity. I have never even looked at the face of a man with lustful thoughts."

Her father, comforting his daughter, went home and organized a wedding ceremony. He gave her to a certain youth who was appropriate for her. After that he wanted to take her to the Buddha to get a blessing for her for a favorable marriage. Taking fragrant flowers and perfume, he went with her to Jeta grove and gave respect to the Buddha. They sat by the side of the Buddha to talk to him. The omnipresent one asked, "Why did you come so late?" And he explained to all a story of what had happened before. The Buddha said, "This girl for a long time has lived with such virtuousness. You not only examined this girl in this life, but in the past also." The father requested the Buddha to tell to him the story of the past and the Buddha did so:

Long ago in the past when King Brahmadatta was ruling in Benares, the Enlightenment Being was born in a forest as a forest deity.

There was a certain man called Greengrocer [Paṇṇika]. The story was the same as today. When he touched the hand of the girl, she said while crying and weeping, "When I was suffering with physical and mental pain you, lord father, were my refuge. At this moment, such a noble father is planning to hurt me in such an unnatural, unwholesome way in the middle of this forest. To whom am I to take refuge by crying when alone in the middle of this forest? The father who was my refuge is now going to do a rough and unusual crime. Because of this saying whose name, to whom can I cry now?" And she cried loudly, calling to the tree deities.

Then that girl's father, consoling her, said, "My little mother. Do not be afraid. You are perfectly fulfilling your purity as a virgin."

Upon hearing this, she said, "Yes, my father. I have indeed fulfilled your desire for me to be a virgin." And the father returned home and arranged a wedding ceremony. He gave her to a very good young man.

Disclosing this incident, the fully enlightened one, the master explained the four noble truths and thus finished the story of Greengrocer

[Paṇṇika]. At the end of the explanation of the four noble truths the father attained the stream entrance state of mind.

The Buddha said, "The daughter at that time was the same as the daughter today. This was seen by me as a tree deity."

The moral: "Once a virtuous person, always a virtuous person."

103

The Story of Hostile Action
(*Veri-Jātaka*)

At one time, the teacher of the three worlds who became the top jewel of the crown of the Sākya clan uttered this story about the millionaire, Anāthapiṇḍika:

The millionaire Anāthapiṇḍika once went to his village where people cultivate for him. On his way back he decided not to stop on the road, having a doubt as to whether there would be robbers on the way, and instead went directly to Sāvatthi. He hurried to Sāvatthi and the next day went to the Buddha and mentioned about his decision to come directly back without stopping.

The omnipresent one said, "Oh, millionaire. Even in the past wise people, seeing robbers on the way, without delaying came directly to the place where they intended to go.

"In an ancient time when King Brahmadatta was ruling in Benares our Enlightenment Being who fulfilled perfections was born in a certain village as a millionaire's son. He was invited by the villagers to stay and take lunch with them, and was delayed because they talked and chatted until evening. When he was returning, he saw some robbers on his way. Seeing them, he hurried on without stopping in the middle of his trip. He ate his dinner at home with the most sumptuous food, lay on his bed and enjoyed himself, saying:

"'What a joy I have achieved. One must come to realize that it is not good to live with a hostile-minded person, wherever he may be, even for a day. If a person lives with such a one even a day, he'll come to live with confusion and unhappiness.'

"Thus the Enlightenment Being enjoying his wisdom performed many meritorious deeds such as the practice of generosity."

Buddha, the master, completed this preaching and ended the story of hostile action.

In those days, the millionaire of Benares was the Buddha.

The moral: "If you expect danger, it is best to avoid it."

104

The Story of Mittavindaka [One Who Enjoys His Friends] (*Mittavinda-Jātaka*)

At one time, the fully enlightened one who is always turning his mind to altruism was in Jetavana monastery. This story was delivered about a certain monk who was disobedient.

The present story is similar to the *Mittavindaka-Jātaka* that was previously spoken [No. 82; and see Nos. 41, 369, and 439]. This Jātaka story was in the time of the Buddha Kassapa. At that time one who was burning in hell and wearing an iron wheel put on his chest as an instrument of torture asked the Enlightenment Being, "Sir. What sort of an unwholesome deed was done by me to suffer like this?" Then the Enlightenment Being explained to him:

You did the following type of unwholesome deed. At one time you saw four divine damsels who were a grouping of temporary hungry ghosts [*vemānika-petī*-s]. Unsatisfied you thought, "Is this enough for happiness or not?" You wondered in such a fashion. You then wondered further, and looked until you saw another eight divine damsels. Without being satisfied by them even, you looked further and saw another twelve divine damsels. And even having seen such a number, you were not satisfied and looked until you saw another sixteen. You were not satisfied even then, and looked further until you saw another thirty-two. And even then you were not satisfied, and being very greedy and dissatisfied you looked even further and then came upon this iron wheel. In this way, without being satisfied with your own luck you kept expecting more and more. Now you have fallen into the trap of an iron wheel. You became enslaved to your cravings, and because of that you are now suffering the torture of the iron wheel cutting your head and giving you terrible pain.

So saying, the Enlightenment Being explained Mittavindaka's pain due to his former deeds.

The Enlightenment Being then went back to his own divine world, and the suffering Mittavindaka had to experience pain in hell for a long time until his previous deeds' power had ended.

Buddha, the master, disclosing this particular story, explained the tale of Mittavindaka. "Mittavindaka was the disobedient monk of today at that time. The Enlightenment Being, who was born as a god at that time, is today myself."

The moral: "Be satisfied even with small achievements. It is not good to be too greedy."

Also,

"Be a gourmet, not a gourmand."

105

The Story of Weak Timber
(*Dubbalakaṭṭha-Jātaka*)

At one time, the fully enlightened one who was the teacher to the whole three worlds with an immense courage was living in Jetavana monastery. He delivered this story about a monk who was very much afraid of death.

A certain young householder who lived in Sāvatthi once listened to the sermon of the Buddha and became very afraid of death. Everywhere he went night and day, whenever he heard a bad noise or the sounds of birds and bees, he fled away while crying loudly with the fear of death, never having reflected on death. If he had reflected on death, he would not have been afraid of death. As he had not practiced mindfulness on death, he was afraid of death. His nature of fearing death spread even among the other monks.

Then the monks, assembled in the hall of the turning of the wheel, brought up a discussion about that monk's fearfulness of death. Buddha, the master, after coming to the preaching hall said, "Oh, monks. What were you talking about before I came to this place?" The monks told him about what they were talking. Then the Lord summoned the fearful monk and asked him, "Oh, Bhikkhu. Is it true that you have become afraid of death?" And the monk answered, "Yes, sir." And the Buddha said:

Oh, monks. Do not look down on this Bhikkhu because he has been afraid of death even before this life.

Long ago in the past, a king called Brahmadatta was ruling in Benares. At that time, the Enlightenment Being who had finished completing his perfections was born in the Himalayan forest as a tree deity.

The king of Benares at that time, wanting to train his royal elephant in war, gave the elephant to elephant trainers. The elephant could not bear the pain of the training. Breaking the rope that was tying him, he ran to the Himalayan forest. People chased after him. They could not catch him, and returned with empty hands.

Since then, the elephant became one who feared death. Even when hearing the sound of the wind blowing, he would become afraid and would run fast while trembling, shaking his trunk. He felt that his four legs were tightened with ropes and that he was being pricked with an elephant goad. Such was the fear he suffered. He used to wander while trembling without having any physical or mental enjoyments.

The tree deities sitting on branches saw him, and one of them said,

"Branches of trees that are weak can be blown down easily by the east and west winds. In this forest, such weak branches are everywhere. If you are afraid of those branches falling down from the wind, it is not good. Eat grass, and drink water, and live happily in this forest."

And when this tree deity addressed him like this, the elephant became brave from that point on.

The master, the fully enlightened one, disclosed this sermon on the law. He preached the four noble truths and spoke this Jātaka story of weak timber.

At the end of the sermon, the monk who was afraid of death attained the stream entrance state of mind. He became a Sotāpanna.

This monk at that former time was the elephant. And the tree deity was the Buddha who has attained full enlightenment today.

The moral: "Fear is mere hallucination."

106

The Story of Infatuation with an Unmarried Girl of Marriageable Age
(*Udañcani-Jātaka*)

While the compassionate Buddha was living in Jetavana monastery, he disclosed this story regarding a monk who was infatuated with an unmarried girl of marriageable age. The incident will come in detail in the Jātaka story of *Culla-Nārada-Kassapa* in the thirteenth book [No. 477].

[There was a girl who thought, "Nobody has asked for me. Therefore it would be good to persuade a monk suitable to me. Then I can ask him to disrobe and be with him. Thinking so, she selected a young monk who was not strongly devoted to monkhood. One day while her mother was preparing food for alms, she saw such an attractive young monk and invited him to her house for alms. There she offered him food. She said to the monk, "Sir, from now on do not go elsewhere for alms. Please come here every day." Since then, he started to go there and he became more familiar with her.

One day her mother said, "There is no one to inherit my wealth at home as I have no son or nephew." On hearing these words, his mind was changed. Her mother said, "Now is the time that you can persuade this monk." And she did it by showing him her feminine wiles. She persuaded him, and he determined to disrobe. He slept with her lust, not with her body. After, though, he went to his teacher and disclosed the situation of his mind and informed his master that he had disrobed. Then the teacher took him to the Buddha. The Buddha told him that he was not only infatuated in this life, but also in a past life.]

The Buddha summoned the monk and asked whether it was true that he had become infatuated with a woman. He said, "Yes, sir." Then the

Buddha asked, "Bhikkhu, with what type of a woman have you become infatuated?" He responded, "Your lordship, I have become infatuated with a woman who has never associated with a man, and who has spent her entire young life alone. Such a person is the one who has attracted my mind."

Then the Buddha said, "Bhikkhu, this woman will bring harm to you. Not only in this life, even in a previous life you have violated you celibate life and wandered trembling on account of her. Because of association with wise people, you again came to happiness." And the Buddha disclosed the story of his past:

Long ago in the past when a king called Brahmadatta ruled in Benares, there was a recluse who was the Bodhisatta who lived in the forest with his son. Once the recluse went out to collect fruit, and he then returned in the evening and saw that his son had done no chores at home. He asked his son, "My son, since we came to this forest you always brought firewood and drinking water and you always made a fire. But today you have done nothing. Why are you so upset?" Then the son said, "My dear father, after you left the hermitage there came a woman who captured my mind. She wants me to go with her, but I did not go thinking that I had to get permission from you first. I made her wait for me on the way. Please give me permission to go now."

On hearing these words the Enlightenment Being thought, "Now it is not easy to stop him." He said, "If so, you can go, son. But whenever this woman bothers you, saying all the time that she would like you to bring her meat, fish, sesame oil, salt, and rice, remind yourself of my meritorious qualities and come back and live here with me." Then the son left for the city with her.

After coming to the city, the woman showed the young man her lures. Whenever she needed something like meat or fish she would persuade him to bring them. He could not refuse her. When she did like this, the son thought, "This woman bothers me requesting this and that, thinking I am a servant." And he became depressed, left her and went back to his father's hermitage.

He paid respect to his father and said, "My honorable father, I lived with you content. I was so infatuated by a woman, I let her lead me away. There, at her home, she bothered me requesting this and that all the time. She used me as if a bucket that would take water from a well, as if a cup that takes water from a jug. This woman was a trickster, deceiving me with sweet words and lustful promises, and by these means fooling me as a young lad to do all her bidding." He detailed all her bad qualities to his father.

Then the Enlightenment Being comforted him and said, "Okay, my son. Come back and stay here. And from now on, think of her with loving kindness and be compassionate toward her." Saying so, he taught him the four sublime states of mind on which to meditate.

The ascetic son developed his mind though that meditation and gained the five knowledges and eightfold concentrations, and lived with his father. In due course of time, he was born in the Brahma realm with his father.

Buddha, the master, disclosed this Dhamma sermon covering the four noble truths, which are the noble truth of unhappiness, the noble truth of the cause for unhappiness, absence of the cause of unhappiness, and the path leading to the attainment of enlightenment. In this way, he finalized the story of this Udañcani, this bucket that would take water from a well. At the end of the preaching, the upset monk attained the stream entrance state of mind. He became a Sotāpanna.

At that time, the unmarried girl of marriageable age was the same as today. The ascetic son was the monk who became upset. The ascetic was the Buddha of the present.

The moral: "Beauty is skin deep."

107

The Story of the Slinging Stone
(*Sālittaka-Jātaka*)

The Buddha who was bringing happiness to people, when he was living at Jetavana monastery, disclosed this story about a certain clever monk and a slingshot.

A certain man in Sāvatthi was skilled in using a slingshot. One day he was listening to the Buddha and he became pleased with the law. Becoming very familiar with the teachings of the Buddha, he became ordained, received higher ordination, and was admitted among the community of monks. Even though he was admitted in the higher ordination of the monks, yet he was not a monk who was devoted too much to the law, and he did not have much respect for the practice of the law.

This monk went one day to take a bath on the bank of the Aciravatī River with a young novice. Meanwhile two white swans were flying in the sky over them. They saw the two swans and the elder Bhikkhu said to the young one, "Shall I put down the swan who is behind by shooting a slinging stone at his eye?"

The young monk said, "How can you put him down? You have no power to put him down by hitting him."

Then the elder monk said, "Young monk, if you like not only can I hit the swan in the eye on this side, but also on the far side."

The young monk thought, "He speaks a lie." And he said, "If so, then do it."

Then the other monk took a small triangular shaped stone and threw it behind the swan. The stone, making a noise, caught the swan's attention. Hearing the sound, the swan thought that there was maybe a danger. Thinking so, it turned to hear the sound better. Then the monk took a round stone and hit the swan in one eye. The stone went out through the other eye, and the swan fell down screaming at their feet.

Thereupon the young monk censured him saying, "You have done a very bad thing." He took him to the Buddha saying, "Sir, this monk has done such a type of bad thing." Then the omnipresent one censured the monk and said, "Oh monks, this man is not only clever in this life with a slingshot, but also was clever in the past too."

Then the Buddha told this story of the past:

At one time, there was a king called Brahmadatta in Benares. Our Enlightenment Being at that time became the minister to the king. At the same time, the king had an advisor Brahmin who was very, very talkative. He was a chatterbox. When he started to speak, he did not let others speak. The king thought, "When will I be able to stop the chatter of this man." And he was thinking of ways to stop this unusual talking of the Brahmin.

In the meantime, there was a certain crippled man who was very clever in slinging stones. Children in the city put this crippled man on a cart, took him near a spreading Banyan tree that was by the city gate, and kept him there under the large shady Banyan tree. They surrounded him, gave him a little bit of money, and asked him to make elephant forms, horse forms, or something like that in the leaves. The crippled man slung stones over the Banyan leaves and he made lion forms, deer forms and bird forms. He made various types of forms. All the leaves of the Banyan tree now had shaped gaps in them.

When the king was on his way to sport in his pleasure garden, he came to this place. The security people sent the children who surrounded the crippled man away. They fled away here and there as the security people hit them. The cripple was unable to move, and he lay under the Banyan tree. When the king came to the Banyan tree and saw that the leaves of the tree were with shaped gaps, and that the shade was no longer perfect, he looked up at the tree sitting on his chariot and saw that all the gaps formed elephant shapes, lion shapes, horse shapes, and the like. He asked, "Who did this?" Then the officers of the king searched and found the crippled man. The king thought, "This man would be a very good help to stop the talkativeness of the Brahmin."

The king's officers saw the crippled man lying down under the tree and said, "Your lordship, here is the man." And they showed him the cripple. The king summoned him and asked all this retinue to go away. He said, "I have a talkative Brahmin in my court. Can you make him silent?" "Your lordship, if I can have a measure of dry goat's dung I can silence him."

The king took the crippled man to his palace, and keeping him behind a curtain that had a hole in its middle, he made a seat in front of that curtain on which he might sit the Brahmin and left the dry goat's dung with the crippled man. When the Brahmin came to the court he was asked to sit on that chair. The Brahmin began to speak.

The Brahmin, without letting anyone else speak, began to talk. The crippled man took the pellets of dry goat's dung one by one and shot them through the hole into the Brahmin's mouth. The Brahmin could not drop them out from deference to the king, and he swallowed them. The dry goat's dung that was about a measure's worth went into his stomach. The king thought, "He may not be able to digest this dry goat's dung." He said, "Hurry up and go home, and bring some leaves of a Piyaṅgu tree with you. Grind them and crush them, drink the juice from that, and vomit. And then be in good health."

The Brahmin kept his mouth shut from that point on.

The king gave presents to the crippled man, thinking, "This man has given me comfort to my ears by making the Brahmin silent." He gave him four villages in each of the four directions, which produced 100,000 gold coins per year.

Then the Enlightenment Being came to the king and said, "Your lordship, education must be obtained by wise people in the world. Even the crippled man, having learned to sling stones and being skilled in this art has gotten such an immense wealth. Therefore, your lordship, look at this crippled man using dry goat's dung who has gotten so much wealth.

The advantage of education is endless." He emphasized again and again the value of learning.

Lord Buddha, the master, disclosed this Dhamma sermon and ended this story of the *Sālittaka-Jātaka* [this Story of the Slinging Stone].

"The cripple at that time was this monk who killed the swan. The king was the Venerable Ānanda. The wise minister was the fully enlightened one who am I, the teacher of the three worlds."

The moral: "Whatever you learn brings you wealth and happiness."

108

The Story of the Woman from Bāhiya State
(*Bāhiya-Jātaka*)

Once Buddha was living in the city of Vesāli in the gabled chamber in the Great Grove. This Dhamma story was delivered about a certain Licchavi king. He was a very pious man, pleased with the law of the Buddha and the community of the monks. He thought: "Buddha is mine. Dhamma [the law] is mine. Saṅgha [the community of the monks] is mine." Constantly, he used to confirm the five precepts without committing any violation. On the full moon days, he observed the higher precepts. One day this king invited the Buddha and the community of monks for lunch, and he especially decorated his palace and performed his Dāna [alms giving] ceremony.

His queen had a very fat body with fat limbs. She was pale like a dead body, and had no beauty. All that she had was fatness and height. After the alms giving, Buddha preached about the advantage of alms giving and gave appreciation in rejoice of their merit.

The Buddha returned home to his own apartment. In the evening, the monks assembled to listen to the Buddha. Before the Buddha's arrival the monks who assembled there started a discussion. And they said, "See, brothers, such a pious and handsome king has no beautiful queen with noble features. Her body was very fat, and she had no physical beauty or merit. How can this king live with such a woman?" They were involved with such a discussion when the Buddha entered.

The master approached the preaching hall and sat on the well-prepared seat as if a sun glittering over Mount Meru's rocks. The Buddha asked, "Monks, in what type of a discussion were you involved before I arrived, and how much more is there to go?" Then the monks said, "Your lordship, in whatever you advised us not to talk about, such as speech about kings and thieves, the thirty-two types of prohibited speech, we were not engaged. We had pious thoughts, such as: 'Buddha is mine. Dhamma is mine. Saṅgha is mine.' With such regard for the triple gem, that handsome Licchavi king was living with an unpleasant-looking fat queen. How can they live together in the palace? We were involved with such talk."

"Monks, not only in the present has this Licchavi king lived with such an unpleasant-looking woman. He has done so even in the past very long ago." And the Buddha kept silent.

Then, one monk out of those assembled monks, making an Añjali[2] with his hands kept up on his head as if a plantain tree fallen down with the heaviness of bananas, knelt down in the presence of the Buddha, prostrated himself before the feet of the Buddha who is endowed with 108 physical beauties, and requested respectfully, "Your lordship, now it is clear to us why in this present life this handsome king is living with this ugly-looking queen. The past story, though, is covered to us as if a spark in ashes. Therefore, please be kind enough to disclose this hidden story to us that is covered as if a gem covered with clay on the ground. We request you to disclose the past story as if taking out the moon from behind a covering dark cloud." Then the Buddha who was requested to speak by the monks disclosed this story of the past:

Long ago in the past there was a king called Brahmadatta in Benares. Our lord the Bodhisatta, the Enlightenment Being, who was fulfilling the ten perfections, became his minister. At that time a certain fat woman who lived in a remote area and who had no particular attractive physical appearance lived by working as a servant. While she was going nearby the palace compound, she wanted to go to the bathroom. As there was no bathroom she did what she had wanted to do outside. She covered her body with a hand cloth. The king was looking at this through the window and thought, "This woman being in such an open place attended to her

---

2 An Añjali is a sign of homage made with one's hands.

needs covering herself with a little piece of cloth so as to avoid fear and shame, and she got up quickly. There is no doubt that she must be a very healthy woman with good physical ability. From such a body, if there be born a son, no doubt he would be a lucky meritorious person. Therefore, it would be good to make her my queen." Then the king, having made such a decision, determined whether or not she was married. Finding out that she was unmarried, he summoned her to the palace, had her sit on a heap of gems and married her, pouring sacred water on her head.

She became very loving to the king, and the king became more and more pleased with her. In due course she delivered a baby boy. After the death of the king, he became a Universal Monarch who was endowed with the seven noble gems and who ruled the whole universe making it one kingdom.

At that time the Enlightenment Being was known as Bāhiya and seeing the prosperity of the woman who came from the Bāhiya state, he thought, "It is good to speak at this time about her to the king." And in a respectful way, he said, "Your lordship, why do not people learn what they have to know about things. This queen who was born in a remote village and who had shame and fear was covering herself with a hand cloth, did her physical needs and achieved the very high position of queen, being first among 16,000 women in the palace. She gave birth to a son who has unlimited fame and prosperity and an immense retinue.

"As the queen came to such prosperity, therefore it is good to learn what we have to know about things from this."

Emphasizing the value of learning good qualities, the Enlightenment Being said,

"Furthermore, your lordship, there are many people in this world who would like to learn writing, reading, mathematics, music, astrology, meter, lexicology, and poetic adornment,[3] and who would like to gain the advantages of having learned these things. However, there are good human qualities that people do not want to learn and follow and many

3 Or, the techniques of poetic composition.

do not know the good results that following such qualities can gain. To understand that, this queen who was born in a remote village and who maintained her cultural values when in an emergency she needed to use the bathroom is a very good example. Following shame and fear she was capable of pleasing your lordship's mind, and came to be the queen of your lordship." And in this fashion, he stated the value and the results of good education.

The lord Buddha, the master, delivered this Dhamma sermon and emphasized the noble truth of suffering, the cause of suffering, the absence of suffering, and the path leading away from suffering, and finalized the story of this *Bāhiya-Jātaka* with the following connection of the story of the past to the present.

"The king at that time was the same king as today, and the queen was the same queen. The minister who advised the king with the Dhamma and how to maintain the well-being of subjects, and who taught good and bad to them, being wise, was I the Lord Buddha."

The moral: "Look deeper than appearances."

109

The Story of a Sweetcake of Husk Powder
(Kuṇḍakapūva-Jātaka)

At one time Buddha was living in Jetavana monastery in Sāvatthi. At that time, many people of Sāvatthi offered alms to the Buddha and the community of monks. Once, a very, very poor man who was even unable to offer alms thought that he should take part in this giving of alms. He had some husk powder, and of it he made a sweetcake. He took it to the monastery thinking that he would give it in person to the Buddha. During the period of alms giving, people first offered gruel, and then said, "Now it would be good to offer sweets." As soon as this was said, the poor man offered his husk powder sweetcake to the Buddha.

Buddha out of compassion accepted it instead of many other sweets, and refusing all other sweets the Buddha consumed it and returned to the Jetavana monastery.

On hearing this news many kings, kings' relatives and ministers went to this man and asked, "Can you give us the merit you acquired? We will pay you." Then the poor man thought, "I acquired this merit with some hardships. Let me go to the Buddha and ask whether I should give it to them." And he went to the Buddha and asked about this. Buddha said, "Both with and without taking money, giving one's merit is good."

After hearing that, he gave merit to everybody in the city. In return he got 900,000 pounds of gold.

The king of Kosala hearing this news conferred upon the poor man the office of treasurer and offered him a white parasol, the mark of his new status.

On this day the monks who had assembled in the Dhamma hall to listen to the evening Dhamma sermon of the Buddha were discussing the news of the poor man's appointment to his new status of treasurer. Buddha went to the Dhamma hall and sat on his well-prepared divan and addressed the monks, asking, "Oh monks, what sort of discussion were you engaged in before my arrival?" The monks said, "Your lordship, we were not discussing any of the thirty-two things with which you asked us not to be involved. We were talking about the high status achieved by the poorest man offering alms to you."

The Buddha said, "Not only now but even before in his previous birth also he achieved such great wealth by offering a husk powder sweetcake." And opening the door to a Jātaka story, he became silent.

One monk out of the community with the assent of all the monks, paying homage to the Buddha, requested, "Your lordship, we know the present story, but we do not know the past story. Therefore we invite your lordship to disclose to us the story which cannot be seen by us, but that can be seen by the Buddha."

Then Buddha uttered the story:

Long ago in the past there was a king in Benares called Brahmadatta who ruled his country righteously. At that time the citizens of Benares ceremoniously worshipped the tree deities with various offerings. One poor person of the city saw a certain castor oil tree, cleared around it, but he had nothing to offer. He saw other people offering to their trees flowers, incense, lights, and foods. He had nothing like that to offer. He thought, "Let me offer my husk powder sweet," and he did so. Then he thought, "Deities eat divine food, ambrosia. How can my deity only eat this husk powder food?" Thinking this, he took back the husk powder sweetcake to eat it himself. The tree deity appeared with a half body in his presence and said, "Oh, man, whatever you get, the same should be gotten by your deity." Hearing this, again he offered the husk powder sweetcake to the deity.

The deity said, "Why do you want to deal with me, a small, weak tree?" The man said, "Your lordship, I am a poor man. So I dealt with you." Then the deity said, "Around this castor oil tree there are treasure pots neck to neck. Dig them all up and show the king those treasure pots. Today you will be conferred the status of treasurer." Saying so, he disappeared.

The poor man did as the deity said. He dug up all the treasure pots and showed them to the king. The king thought, "It would be good to confer upon him the office of treasurer as he has such wealth." And he conferred on him the office of treasurer. The man, having gained such wealth, practiced generosity by giving and acquired a great deal of merit. Finally, he passed away according to his deeds.

Buddha preached this Jātaka story comparing both the present and past.

"The poor man at that time was this poor man. The deity of the castor oil tree was I, the Buddha."

The moral: "Everything has value. No offering with good intentions is too little."

110

The Dilemma Regarding All [Fragrances] Mixed
(*Sabbasaṃhāraka-Pañha*)

This is set out at length in the *Mahā-Ummagga-Jātaka* [No. 546].

[At one time the Enlightenment Being was born as Mahosadha, the great erudite. Before going to see King Videha of the city of Mithilā, he was asked to solve several questions by the citizens of his town. The following is one of those questions.]

Once, a poor woman made a beautiful necklace by tying knots using green, yellow, and red threads. One day when she was going on a journey, she came to the tank that the erudite Mahosadha had made for the benefit of the public. On seeing its beauty and clean water, she decided to take a bath.

With the intention of taking a bath, she took off her necklace and placed it on top of her clothing. She then went down to the tank and began to bathe. Meanwhile, a young girl was walking nearby. She saw this beautiful necklace made from the colored threads. On seeing it, a desire for it grew up within her. She picked it up and asked, "Oh, auntie. This necklace is very beautiful. Who made this? I would like to make one for myself also. Can I put it around my neck and see whether it fits?" Asking so, the older woman who owned the necklace and who was not cunning said, "Yes. See how it fits you." The younger woman, putting it around her neck, ran off.

The older woman who owned the necklace saw that the younger woman was fleeing away. She came out of the water, put on her clothes, and chased after the woman who was fleeing. She ran and caught her, and asked, "Where are you taking my necklace?" Saying so, she held onto her necklace. The other woman shouted and said, "What? I did not take your necklace. This is mine. I have had it for a long time." They started to quarrel. On hearing this quarreling, many people came to see what the problem was.

In the meantime, the Enlightenment Being Mahosadha was playing nearby. He heard the quarreling noise of those two women. Hearing this noise, the Enlightenment Being summoned them both and asked, "Why are you quarreling on the road?" The Enlightenment Being, seeing the two women, realized immediately which one was guilty and which one was innocent. Knowing this, he asked about the cause of the quarrel. When they stated the reason, he asked, "If I settle your dispute, would you agree with my decision or not?" They said, "Yes, we will accept your decision."

When they agreed, the Enlightenment Being first asked the young woman who had stolen the necklace, "What type of a perfume was applied on this necklace by you before you put it on?" The woman said, "Your lordship, I always perfume this necklace with a mixture of many different fragrances, which is known as Sabbasaṃhāraka." Then he asked the other woman, who was the necklace's owner, and she said, "Your lordship, I am a very poor woman. I do not have such a costly perfume. I always perfume it with a fragrance from Piyaṅgu flowers."

The erudite ordered a plate of water to be brought, and he put the necklace in the water. After that, he summoned a perfume-maker and asked him, "What fragrance is in this water? Please smell it and tell me." The perfume-maker said, after smelling it, "Your lordship, in this water I smell the fragrance of the Piyaṅgu flower."

Then, it was found that the young cunning girl was lying, and the old woman was the truthful speaking person.

The Enlightenment Being, Mahosadha, showed the water to the people who gathered around and asked the young woman in their presence, "Tell us now, did you steal it or not?" She said, "Yes, I stole it."

This story was spread throughout the country, and the popularity of Mahosadha in this way also spread throughout the country.

The moral: "Common sense can conquer guile."

111

The Question about the Donkey
(*Gadabha-Pañha*)

This is set out at length in the *Mahā-Ummagga-Jātaka* [No. 546]. [When the Enlightenment Being was born in the city of Mithilā while King Videha was ruling the country, King Videha had four erudites who advised him. King Videha, on hearing of the erudition of the Enlightenment Being, wanted to summon him to the palace. The four erudites were disturbed on hearing this news, and they prevented the invitation from being made because they were jealous. But on hearing further the splendor of the erudition of the Enlightenment Being, Mahosadha, the king without informing his four erudite ministers decided to go alone to see the Enlightenment Being.

On this journey, the king's royal horse, stepping on an uneven area in the road, broke its leg. The king had to come back. When he returned to the palace, the four erudite ministers asked, "Your lordship, did not you go to see and bring back the erudite Mahosadha?" The king said, "Yes." The ministers said, "We asked you not to go there. But without listening to us you wanted to go. See what happened to your horse? Do not be in a hurry." The king had nothing to say, and he kept silent.

After a while, the king again suggested to the ministers that they invite the erudite Mahosadha to the palace. The ministers saw that this time, they could not prevent the king from inviting him.

They said, "Your lordship, if it is so, this time you should not go to him. Last time when you were trying to go to him, your royal horse broke its leg. Therefore, this time, send him a messenger saying, 'Last time when we were trying to come to see you, our horse's leg got broken. Therefore, send us a noble horse (*assatara*)[4] or a nobler one.' If he understands our puzzle, if he sends a noble horse he will come himself. If he sends a nobler one, he will send his father." The king agreed to do so. Sending a messenger, he did as they agreed.]

The Enlightenment Being, Mahosadha, on hearing the message of the king, thought, "Our lord king is willing to see myself and my father." And he went to his father, offered him respect, and said, "Father, our lord king would like to see you and me. Therefore, you go first with a thousand other people. Also, do not go empty-handed. Take with you a good box of fresh ghee. When you go there, the king will ask you to sit down in an appropriate chair. Then you may sit in that appropriate chair. While you and the king are talking to each other, I will arrive. Then the king will greet me and talk to me, and will request that I sit in an appropriate seat. When I look at your face, by that sign, you will get up from your seat and say to me, 'My son, Mahosadha. Sit on this seat.' Then it will be a puzzle *for them*."

The millionaire father accepted what his son said, and as his son had requested, he went first. He arrived near the gate of the palace. The king summoned him. When he entered the palace, he greeted the king, and the king asked, "Where is your son, Mahosadha?" Then he said, "Your lordship, he will come later."

The king became very happy on hearing that Mahosadha was on his way. The king requested the father to take a seat. The father sat down on an appropriate seat.

The Enlightenment Being, Mahosadha, endowed with beautiful clothes and ornaments, surrounded by a thousand other young princes, went into the city of Mithilā. On the edge of the city, he saw a young donkey grazing on the grass along the ditch around the city proper. He ordered his men to catch him and take him with them in such a fashion that the donkey could not make any noise. At the same time, he instructed them not to let anyone at the palace see the donkey. The young men, hearing the Enlightenment Being's words, did everything as he advised.

4 Punningly, a mule (the offspring of a donkey with a common horse).

The Enlightenment Being, Mahosadha, went to the palace of the king with such a large retinue as if he were the king of the gods.

A crowd gathered to see the millionaire's son, Mahosadha, on his way to the palace. The people were saying to each other, "Look! He is the prince born to this world carrying a lump of medicine in his hand. He is the erudite prince who solved such a large number of questions and puzzles sent by the king. Look at his splendor." And they were appreciating the Enlightenment Being, but yet were still not satisfied by seeing him.

The Enlightenment Being reached near the gate of the palace and sent a message with the gatekeeper about his arrival. On hearing the news, the king immediately asked him to come. The Enlightenment Being went with his retinue, made his respects to the king, and kept aside while standing. The king became very happy and talked pleasantly to him. He said, "Erudite Mahosadha, be seated in an appropriate seat."

Then, the Enlightenment Being, Mahosadha, looked at his father's face. By that sign, the millionaire father got up from his seat and said, "Erudite, take this seat." When Mahosadha's father said this, immediately Mahosadha sat down on his father's seat.

On seeing Mahosadha take his father's seat and sit on it, the four erudite ministers and other wise people, clapping their hands, loudly started to laugh. They laughed, saying, "It is said that this prince is a wise person. But he is an unwise person." The king became very upset, and was silent.

Then the Enlightenment Being asked the king, "Your lordship, are you worried?" The king said, "Yes, erudite. I am worried. On hearing about your nature, I became happy. But on seeing it, I have become unhappy and worried." Mahosadha said, "What is the reason for being happy on hearing about my nature, but unhappy on seeing it." The king said, "Because you made your father get up from his seat, and you sat in your father's seat."

Mahosadha said, "Tell me, your lordship, do you say that fathers are always more noble than sons?" The king said, "Yes, erudite." Then the Enlightenment Being said, "Your lordship, you requested me to send a noble horse [*assatara*] or a nobler one. Saying so, he got up from his seat and requested his retinue to bring the donkey near to the king. Keeping the donkey near the king's feet, he said, "Your lordship, what is the value of this donkey?" The king said, "If it is working, it will be worth nearly eight gold coins." Then the Enlightenment Being asked, "How much is the value of a noble horse [*ājāniya-sindhava*] that is in the womb of a mare impregnated by this one?" The king said, "Erudite, it is invaluable." Then Mahosadha said, "Your lordship, why do you say so? Just now you said that the father is always nobler than the son. If it is true, in your words, the donkey is more valuable than the noble horse. Look, your lordship. Your erudites do not understand even such a little thing. They clapped their hands and laughed at me. The knowledge of your erudites is amazing! From where did you pick out your erudites?" Saying so, he put those scholiasts in their place. And he said further to the king, "Your lordship, if you think that the father is always nobler than the son, you can take my father for your service in the royal office. If sons can be nobler than their fathers, take me into your service in the royal office."

The king became very happy. All the people assembled there applauded, showing their appreciation for his having explained the riddle so well. They all shouted, "Well done! Well done!" And they waived their shawls above their heads in a circular fashion. The four erudites, Senaka and the others, could not say anything as they had been defeated and shamed.

There is no being who can understand the value of parents better than the Enlightenment Being. The reason he asked his father to get up from his seat and then sat in that same seat was not to belittle his father. The king had sent him a riddle requesting him to send a noble horse or a nobler one. To solve that riddle, and to convince the gathered assembly that he was wiser than the erudites present, he had to belittle those erudites.

The moral: "Wisdom can change even the position of noble and nobler."

112

The Dilemma of Princess Amarā [The Dilemma of the Hidden Road, The Dilemma of the Maiden]

(*Amarādevī-Pañha, Channapatha-Pañha, Strī-Pañha*)

This dilemma will be found too in the *Mahā-Ummagga-Jātaka* [No. 546]. [When the Enlightenment Being was born as the erudite Mahosadha, he was given a number of riddles to solve by the populace. Then he was summoned to the royal palace, where he took up residence. While living there and serving the king, he became sixteen years of age and grew into a handsome youth.]

The king's queen, Queen Udumbara, thought, "The Enlightenment Being, who is like a brother, has become a youth. He has plenty of wealth. Now it is time to bring an appropriate wife from a family of similar rank. She mentioned this to the king. On hearing this news, the king became very happy and said, "That is good, indeed, my sweetheart. Tell him the news."

The queen told this to the Enlightenment Being. He accepted the proposal. She asked him, "Brother, if such is the case, shall we bring princesses that are appropriate to your standing from different places?" The Enlightenment Being thought, "The maidens brought to me by her may not fulfill my requirements. Therefore, first I will go and find someone myself who is appropriate." He said, "Your grace, I will go away for a few days and look myself for a suitable wife. Do not tell the king the reason I have gone away. I will select a maiden whom I like, and I will inform you first. The queen agreed, saying, "Yes, my younger brother. Do as you like." The Enlightenment Being, after kneeling in front of her, went back to his residence. He informed his friends and household of his impending journey and its purpose. Disguised as a tailor, and taking a tailor's tools, he left alone through the northern gate and set out for the central northern village.

At that time, there was a poor family that had been wealthy in the past. All who had seen the only daughter in that family considered her to be beautiful. She was endowed with all female charms and virtues owing to her merits in her past lives. She was beautiful like a female form drawn on a cloth.

One morning, she was carrying gruel to her father who was ploughing the family's field. She set forth on the same road on which the Enlightenment Being was walking. When he saw her approach, he thought, "This girl is beautiful, and is endowed with all female charms. If she does not have a husband, she would make a good wife for me."

The maiden Amarā, on seeing the Enlightenment Being, thought, "If I can have such a one as my husband, I may be able to bear a noble family that can earn much wealth and thereby restore the wealth of my family."

The Enlightenment Being thought, "As I do not know whether or not she has a husband, I will question her with a hand gesture. If she is wise enough to understand my hand gesture, she will reply." Thinking so, he made his hand into a fist and raised it, while still at a distance from her.

On seeing this, Amarādevī thought, "This man asked me whether or not I have a husband." She spread out her fingers. The Enlightenment Being understood that she was unmarried, and approaching her, he asked, "Damsel, what is your name?" "Master, if there be one in this world who never existed in the past, never exists in the future, and who is not now existing, that is my name."

Then he said, "Dear maiden, as there is no immortal being [*amara*] in the world, your name should be Amarā. Is that so?"

She said, "Yes, sir."

And he asked, "To whom are you carrying this gruel?"

She said, "I am carrying it to my foremost god."

Then he said, "Ah, you are carrying gruel to your father?"

She said, "Yes, sir."

And he asked, "What is your father doing?"

"He is making one thing into two."

"To make one thing into two is to plough. Is he ploughing, dear?"

"Yes, sir."

"Where is your father ploughing?"

She said, "Sir, if somebody goes to a place and he or she does not return, he is ploughing in such a place."

Then he said, "If somebody goes somewhere, and he or she does not come back from there, such a place is a cemetery. Is he ploughing at a cemetery?"

Then she said, "Yes, sir."

Then Mahosadha asked her, "My dear, will you come back today or tomorrow?"

Then she said, "Sir, if it comes, I will not come. If it does not come, then I will come."

Then the Enlightenment Being said, "Beautiful one, does your father plough on the other side of a river? Because from what I understand, you said that if the river floods you will not be able to come. And if it does not flood, then you will come."

Then she said, "Yes, my lord."

This is the discussion they had. Amarādevī requested him to accept some gruel, saying, "Sir, would you like some gruel?"

The Enlightenment Being thought, "It is not good to reject this first invitation." And he said, "Alright. I would like to drink a little."

Then she took the container down from on top of her head and placed it on the ground. The Enlightenment Being thought, "If she hands me gruel without washing the cup and offering me water first, then I will leave her here and will go."

But Amarādevī rinsed the cup, filled it with water that she offered to him, and then took back the empty cup. She placed it on the ground instead of leaving it in his hand, stirred the container of gruel, filled the cup with gruel, and then gave it back into his hand.

As it happened, there was very little rice in the gruel. The Enlightenment Being said, "My dear, when the rice was growing in your field, it did not get enough water. [Because of this, it has not puffed up in the cooking.]"

She said, "Yes, sir."

Amarādevī, leaving enough gruel for her father, fed the Enlightenment Being sufficiently with gruel.

After drinking the gruel, he washed his mouth and said, "Sweet lady, I would like to go to your home. Tell me the way."

Then she said, "Very well. Go this way into the inner village and then you will see a restaurant where they sell Aggala.[5] Pass it, and go further ahead. Then you will see a restaurant where they sell gruel. Pass that too and go further ahead, and you will see a coral tree in full blossom. When you reach that tree, take the road that turns toward the hand with which you eat. Do not take the road that turns toward the hand with which you do not eat. In other words, do not go left. Turn right, and go further. Then you will see our Middle Village where my parents' house is. In a roundabout way I am telling you the way to my parents' home."

The moral: "Both men and women can be wise."

5 Aggala is balls of dough made of flour mixed with sugar.

113

The Story of the Jackal
(*Sigāla-Jātaka*)

This story was delivered by the Buddha when he was in Veḷuvanārāma monastery in the city of Rājagaha about 500 newly ordained monks who were led astray by the elder Devadatta. They lived making a monastery on the bank of the river Gayāsīsa. Devadatta was declaring that Buddha did not do the proper discipline. Saying so, he lived a separate life with the 500 monks.

One day in the evening the monks were discussing about Devadatta's hypocritical life. While they were discussing this, Buddha came to the preaching hall, sat on the Buddha-seat and asked, "Oh monks, what were you talking about before I came here?" They said, "Sir, we were talking about Devadatta's creation of schism." The Buddha said, "Not only today, even in the past he was a liar." Then the monks asked the Buddha to disclose the previous story. Buddha declared the past story:

Once in the past when king Brahmadatta was touring Benares there was a New Year's Day festival declared in the city. People offered food items such as toddy, meat and the like food varieties as sacrifice to the deities everywhere in the street. On the very same night there came a certain jackal into the city, smelling the food items. He greedily ate as much as he could. As he was intoxicated, he lay down on the side of a road and could not leave before dawn. When dawn arrived he thought, "At this time it is not good to go." He hid by the side of a small bush. While he was looking at the road he saw a solitary Brahmin, and thought, "Brahmins are very greedy. I want to deceive this Brahmin and leave this place under his protection." He came to the Brahmin and said, "Friend, if you can take me out of this city, I can show you where 200 gold coins are hidden." The

Brahmin thought, "The jackal is trustworthy." He covered the jackal with his upper cloth, took him under his armpit and went out from the city. He said to the jackal, "Show me the wealth." The jackal said, "Go a little farther, and I'll show you." And he took him to a cemetery and said, "Here is the wealth. Put me down and spread your upper shawl on the ground." He said, "Dig under that tree." While the Brahmin was digging under the tree, the jackal defecated and urinated in the middle and in each of the four corners of the shawl, and ran away. Then while he was digging the ground, the tree deity came out from this tree and said, "Oh foolish Brahmin, what you have done is trust a jackal who has deceived you. That jackal had not even 200 seashells. By trusting him, what you have gained is the soiling of your cloth. Foolish Brahmin, go, have a bath and wash your cloth, and do your own religious works." The Brahmin did this, going back home.

The jackal at that time was Devadatta, and the tree deity was I, the Buddha.

The moral: "Never trust a liar."

114

The Story of a Proper Thinking Fish
(*Mitacinti-Jātaka*)

At one time when Buddha was living at Jetavana monastery the Buddha disclosed this story about two old monks. These two old monks went to observe rainy season retreat in a remote village. Their donors there offered them all necessary requisites as much as they wanted.[6] The two monks enjoyed the three months of the rainy season retreat. As it was so comfortable there, they stayed there continuously without coming to see the Buddha through the next rainy season as well. And after that they left for the city of Sāvatthi to see the Buddha.

Upon seeing these two monks, the other monks who were friends of theirs questioned, "Why did you Venerable ones delay in coming to see the Buddha?" They said, "It was very good where we were. It was comfortable because everything was available to us there. So we were there for a second rainy season also."

On that day, all the elderly monks assembled to listen to the Buddha's evening Dhamma sermon were talking about this matter regarding the failure of these monks in coming to see the Buddha.

When the Buddha came in and sat on his prepared seat, addressing the monks, he asked, "Oh monks, what were you talking about before I came in?" And the monks said, "Venerable sir, we were talking about those two old monks and their laziness to fulfill their monks' duties after the termination of the rainy season retreat."

Then the Buddha said, "Monks, not only today, but also formerly they both were lazy." And then the monks invited him to disclose the

6 The four requisites of a monk are food, clothing, shelter, and medicine.

story of old about these two monks' laziness. The Buddha disclosed the following:

In an ancient time, there was a king called Brahmadatta ruling Benares. At that time, upstream in the river there were three fish known as Thinking-Too-Much, Thinking-Little, and Proper-Thinking. They were living close to a village where people lived. One day Proper-Thinking said, "We live close to people. It is dangerous to live so close to them. Therefore, let us go somewhere else." The other two fish said, as they were greedy and liked eating the plentiful food that was upstream, craving it, "Let us go today or tomorrow." And saying so, they postponed their departure. They spent over three months without leaving.

One day fishermen came and spread their nets across the river. The two fish, Thinking-Too-Much and Thinking-Little, carelessly swimming ahead did not smell the net. And they got trapped in it. Proper-Thinking, swimming behind, smelled the net and went through the far side. He did not get trapped in it. Seeing the other two foolish fish, he thought, "They did not listen to me. Not listening to me, but instead going boldly and greedily, they got trapped in the net. It is my duty to save them." Thinking this, he performed a trick by going out of one side of the net and into the other side, splashing. The fishermen thought, as big fish were trapped in the net, "No doubt the net has been torn as there were many big fish trapped in it." And they hauled in the net by one side, and took it up. When they took it up, these two fish easily escaped. All three were saved.

The Buddha, connecting this old story to the present incident, explained the disadvantages of craving. He preached, expressing the four noble truths. Listening to this particular Dhamma sermon of the Buddha, these two old monks attained the stream entrance state of mind, which is endowed with a thousand different ways of understanding the law, becoming Sotāpanna-s.

"The two fish, Thinking-Too-Much and Thinking-Little, were these two monks at that time. And the Proper-Thinking fish was I who have become the Buddha today."

The moral: "Proper thinking leads you to success and happiness. Procrastination due to greed leads to ruin."

115

The Story of a Bird
[The Story of a Bird That Warned Others]
(*Sakuṇa-Jātaka, Anusāsika-Jātaka*)

At one time the all-knower was living in Sāvatthi. This story was spoken about a certain housewife who was ordained among the sisters and who was too fond of food. Once she went collecting alms on a certain street, and there she was well entertained by the devoted people who offered her the daintiest food. She thought, "Let no other nun come to collect alms in this street. If such were to happen, I might miss these well-prepared entertainments." Therefore she thought further, "I must prevent other nuns from coming to this street." Thinking so, she returned to the nunnery and told the other nuns, "On such-and-such a street there are elephants, horses, biting dogs, and other harmful animals. It is not good for anyone to go there." The other nuns who heard this, believed what she said as the truth. They completely kept away from going to that street. They even did not want to look at that place.

Then, only that nun went to that street for alms. One day she went there to a house for alms. While she was going toward the house, a certain ram ran after her and attacked her. Her thighbone was broken. The people who were in the vicinity came about her and set her thighbone with a bandage. They put her on a stretcher and took her to the nunnery.

This news was spread among the monks and nuns in the temple. On that occasion, when the Buddha came to the preaching hall in the evening and sat on the prepared platform, he asked the monks, "Oh monks, what were you talking about before I came here?" They said, "Venerable sir, we were discussing about the nun who broke her thighbone in the street."

And they related the story. The Buddha said, "Not only in this life by warning others falsely did she have to face the problem of a broken bone, but also in the past she faced death." And then the disciples invited him to disclose the past story.

Buddha said:

Long ago in Benares when a king called Brahmadatta ruled, the Enlightenment Being was born as a king of birds. In his flock of birds, one female bird got plenty of food. And while she was eating this food, one day she thought, "If other birds come to this location, I will lose this plentiful fare. It is better not to let them come." Thinking this way, she went back to the flock and said, "That road is packed with lots of bullocks which pull chariots, and with many other troublesome animals. It is not good to go there as it is dangerous."

Hearing this, other birds never wanted to go there.

As she was wandering as was her wont in that location by herself, a fast chariot came up behind her. She turned her neck and saw the chariot coming up behind, but neglected to get out of the way as she was greedily eating food and thought the chariot was far off. Unfortunately, when the chariot came near her, she could not fly off. She was cut into two pieces, and died. The Enlightenment Being while flying overhead in the sky, asked the other birds, "Where is that female bird who was warning others?" And they saw her dead on the road. The Enlightenment Being said, "Look at her. She died being enslaved to her own craving. Because of that, she is dead in vain." They went away, leaving her body behind.

The female bird at that time that was warning others was the present nun. And the king of the birds at that time was I who became the enlightened one.

The moral: "It is not good to be greedy."

Further,

"False admonitions to others have a way of befalling oneself."

116

The Story of Disregarded Advice
(*Dubacca-Jātaka*)

Once the omniscient one was living in Jetavana monastery. He disclosed this Jātaka story regarding a certain monk who disregarded counsel. This Jātaka story comes in detail in the *Gijjha-Jātaka* in the ninth book [No. 427].

[A monk was ordained, and after his ordination he became disregardful of his teacher's advice. He did not follow the precepts and religious practices properly. The elderly monks advised him on many things. He thought, "Why should I be obedient to these elders? I know what to do and what to say." And he became more and more disrespectful to the elder monks. This was heard by the Buddha, and the Buddha summoned him and said, "Oh monk, you even in the past became disobedient and destroyed your life."]

Addressing the monks, the omniscient one said, "Oh monks, this monk not only disregarded counsel in this life, but also did so in the past." And then the monks in the audience requested the Buddha to express the hidden past. The Buddha then spoke this story:

At one time when King Brahmadatta ruled Benares, the Enlightenment Being was born in a family of gymnasts. When he became old enough, he learned how to do somersaults. With his master, he went from village to village displaying gymnastics. Once they came to a certain village and prepared to display their skills. While they were preparing the show, the master set up five javelins instead of four as usual. The pupil asked, "Master, why did you set up five javelins instead of four. It is dangerous to have five. Take one javelin out." Then the master, as he was intoxicated, said, "Do you not understand my skills?" Saying so, he did somersaults over the javelins. Over the first four javelins, he jumped safely. But he was not skilled enough to clear the fifth javelin, and impaled himself on it, and died.

The student became very sad, and said, "My master died without listening to my advice." He removed him from the javelin, and cremated him.

Buddha disclosed this story, comparing the past story to the present.

"The gymnast who disregarded advice was the monk in the present. And I who am the Buddha today was born his student at that time."

The moral: "Good advice deserves everyone's attention."

117

The Story of the Partridge
(*Tittira-Jātaka*)

When Buddha was living in Jetavana monastery, the Venerable Devadatta's right hand disciple Kokālika caused a disruption among the monks. Because of that, the Buddha related this Jātaka story. The story of its cause is detailed in the thirteenth book in the *Takkāriya-Jātaka* [No. 481].

[During a certain spring retreat the two chief disciples of the Buddha, Sāriputta and Moggallāna, went to the monk called Kokālika and said, "With your help to us, and with our help to you, we can live together happily in this temple for this rainy season period of three months." The two chief disciples said this so as to try to avoid being bothered by the public. Kokālika asked, "What is the happiness that you can gain because of me?" The two chief disciples said, "If you do not disclose to anyone that we are here, then we can live happily. That is the help you can give us. During these three months, we will teach you the discourses (*sutta*-s) and the philosophical and psychological analyses (*abhidhamma*) of the Buddha. This is how we can help you."

Then the Venerable Kokālika prepared shelter for them. This was not known to anyone. At the end of the rainy season retreat, they requested Kokālika to visit the Buddha with them. On the way to seeing the Buddha, they came to a certain village. After the two chief disciples left the village, the Venerable Kokālika came back and said to the villagers, "You devotees are ignorant like animals. Our chief disciples were with me nearby for the last three months. And now, these two have left to go back to Sāvatthi."

Hearing this, the villagers became very upset and taking many offerings chased after the two chief disciples. Meeting them, they begged pardon and said, "Bhante, we could not recognize you. Please pardon us and accept these offerings." Then the chief disciples refused to accept the gifts and instructed the villagers even not to give them to Kokālika. The villagers invited the two chief disciples to come back again to the village. Kokālika thought, "The chief disciples did not accept these gifts, and they did not even allow me to accept them." And he became angry with them.

The two chief disciples, in Sāvatthi with the Buddha for a short time, again left this time with their 500 disciples to go to the village where Kokālika lived. The villagers treated them with the four requisites of monks (food, clothing, shelter, and medicine). Those monks who went with the two chief disciples shared all the gifts given by the villagers with each other, and did not give any to Kokālika.

Because of this, Kokālika got angry and said, "Both Sāriputta and Moggallāna have bad motives. They did not accept the gifts given before by the villagers when they were here alone. Now they are accepting them when they are together with a retinue of 500 monks." And he accused the two chief disciples in this way, with an evil mind.

However, hearing this the two chief disciples thought, "Kokālika acquires a great amount of demerit because of us. Therefore it is not good to stay here. So, let us go." And they left the place along with their retinue.

Seeing this, the villagers started to cry and plead with them to stay. But they were firm in their decision. Meanwhile, a young monk spoke to the villagers and said, "Oh villagers, how can the two chief disciples stay here without the consent of Kokālika?"

The villagers got angry and went to Kokālika and requested, "Go, please, and invite the Venerable two chief disciples to stay here and beg their pardon. If not, you must leave this village." Then he became afraid of the villagers and requested the two chief disciples to stay. The two chief disciples said, "You, monk, do not go. You stay here. But we will not come back."

Kokālika returned, but he could not stay in the village without the help of the villagers. He became very melancholy and taking his robes and books, left to see the Buddha who was in Jetavanārāma. He complained, "Your lordship, Sāriputta and Moggallāna have bad motives. They have gone over to earning gifts." The Buddha said, "Kokālika, do not say so. They both are very highly virtuous and are endowed with good qualities."

Then Kokālika said, "Sir, your chief disciples' words are unwholesome. I know it. And they are not virtuous." In this way, while Buddha was objecting to his saying so, he left.

Within a short time, everywhere on his body there developed big boils which started to bleed and fester. He could not bear the pain, and screaming lay down near the gate of Jetavanārāma. His bad reputation spread everywhere, even up to the Brahmaloka.

This was seen by a certain higher deity (*brahma*) named Tudu who thought, "It is my duty now to go and advise Kokālika to beg pardon for his fault." Staying in the sky, he said, "Kokālika, you have done a very bad deed. Go hurry up and beg pardon." Then Kokālika asked, "Who are you, sir?" And Tudu said, "I am Tudu, your former master." "What? You are a non-returner to this world? If so, how can you come from the Brahmaloka to this human world? No doubt, you are like a hungry ghost who comes to a heap of garbage." Then the deity went back to his place saying, "If you speak so, then you look out for yourself." And he left. And Kokālika died because of the same disease, and was born in a woeful state called the Hell of Paduma. The Sahāmpati Brahma deity saw this and informed the Buddha. On this occasion, Buddha said, "Kokālika not only in this life, but also in the past, faced difficulties because of his words."]

Buddha stated that the monk Mahā-Kokālika, by speaking too much, faced death even in the past. The monks requested him to disclose the story. The Buddha explained it thus:

At one time, when a king called Brahmadatta reigned in Benares, the Enlightenment Being was born in a well-known Brahmin family of Benares. After growing up, he became ordained as a Ṛṣi. He became the head of many ascetics, and lived in a Himalayan forest.

Then, a certain ascetic who was malnourished, taking an axe, went into the forest to cut firewood so as to warm the hermitage.

Another ascetic came to where he was, and told him, "Cut this, cut this, and cut that." In this way, he was ordering the first ascetic how to cut the wood. The first ascetic got angry and said, "Are you my teacher, that you are teaching me to cut firewood?" He picked up his sharp axe and he slashed him, killing him.

The Enlightenment Being, hearing the news, made all necessary rites and rituals for the dead ascetic. Meanwhile, near the hermitage where the Enlightenment Being was living, there was a certain partridge that was crying loudly on a fruit tree. A partridge hunter, hearing its cries, caught him and killed him. The Enlightenment Being, not hearing its cries for a few days, asked, "What happened to that partridge that cried up until a few days ago?" The other ascetics told him what happened. On hearing this, the Enlightenment Being compared the stories of the dead ascetic and the partridge. Both clamored uselessly. And he advised his fellow ascetics to meditate. He himself meditated on the fourfold sublime statuses of the mind, and gained rapturous ecstasies [*jhāna*-s]. Without failing to maintain those achievements, he was born among the Brahma beings.

Buddha finished this story saying, "At that time, the ascetic who got slashed in the head by the axe was the elder Kokālika. The Ṛṣi who became the head of the group of ascetics was myself, the Buddha."

The moral: "Useless speech brings danger."

118

The Story of the Quail
(*Vaṭṭaka-Jātaka*)

When the enlightened one was living in Jetavana monastery, this Jātaka story was delivered regarding the millionaire called Uttara.

While the millionaire Uttara was living in the city of Sāvatthi, a certain very highly meritorious prince was conceived in his wife's womb, and after ten months he was delivered. He grew up and became a youth.

At one time, there was a Kattikā festival. Many millionaires' children came out with their wives onto the streets and celebrated in the streets for seven days. Uttara also, thinking his son should celebrate with them, went to him and told him of his intentions, saying, "You also go, along with the young women of the household, and celebrate the Kattikā festival."

As the son of Uttara came from the Brahma world, he did not do as his father wished. Thereupon, without his consent, his friends got together and summoned a certain prostitute from the village. She, decorated with ornaments and fancy clothes, tried to entice him. But, on seeing her, he did not want to have anything to do with her. His friends tried to persuade him, letting her show him her feminine wiles, but he only smiled.

The millionaire Uttara's son, looking at her with a distracted mind, saw her as bones only. Seeing her as impurities, he was averse to her. But he thought, "Why should I send her back empty-handed?" So, he gave her all that she needed. She left, and while she was walking in the street, a certain rich official saw her. He led her to his home.

When the Kattikā celebration was over, the prostitute's mother did not see her daughter. She went to the millionaires' sons and accused them of taking her daughter. She asked, "Where is she now? Show me." Hearing her accusation, the youths said, "We sent her, on the very same day she was summoned, to the millionaire Uttara's son. Go and ask him." Then she went to him and asked about her daughter. He said, "I sent her away, on the very same day. I do not know where she went." The woman took him to court, and cried before the king. The king examined the case and said, "If she was in your house, you will have to produce her." The young millionaire's son said, "Sir, I do not know where she is."

The king then said, "If it is so, I will order you to be punished." And he did so.

The ministers, hearing the king's order, put cuffs around the millionaire Uttara's son's hands and led him away as punishment drums were beating. On hearing this noise, many people came and surrounded him crying and weeping. They said, "Such a punishment has fallen on such a virtuous person as you!"

The millionaire's son, who was the victim, thought, "If I get rid of this punishment, I will be ordained as a monk in the monastic order of the Buddha."

Meanwhile, the prostitute heard the news that he was sentenced to death because of her. Knowing this, she came from the official's mansion where she had been staying and appeared before the executioners. Some people in the crowd, who saw her, handed her over to her mother. Then, the millionaire Uttara's son was released.

The millionaire's son after being freed from death went to the lake and washed his hair, taking a bath. He then ate rice. After that, he paid respect to his parents, and obtained permission from them to become ordained as a monk. And he went to the forest. He became a monk, and received his higher ordination [*upasampadā*]. Within a few days, gaining insight from meditation, he obtained the status of Arahant.

On the very same day, the elders assembled in the preaching hall were talking about him. When the Buddha entered, he asked the monks, "Oh monks, what were you talking about before I came here?" When they mentioned that the story of the millionaire's son and his attainment of the status of Arahant was being discussed by them, the Buddha said, "Oh monks, not only today but even in the past wise people have been released from death's grip as was this monk today." The Buddha was invited to disclose the story of the past. The Buddha then disclosed this story:

Long ago a king called Brahmadatta was ruling in Benares. At that time, the Enlightenment Being was born among quails. A certain quail hunter in Benares at one point went to the forest and came back having caught a lot of quails. Keeping them at home and feeding them, he sold them to people.

One day, the quail that was the Enlightenment Being got trapped in the net placed down by the quail hunter. He also was brought to the hunter's home. The quail hunter gave the quails that he had caught food to eat to make them fat. But the Enlightenment Being did not eat the food, thinking, "If I eat I will be fat, and I will not be able to escape through the small holes of the net which is confining me." The quail hunter, seeing that this quail was not eating over a few days, took him into his hand and examined him in the palm of his hand so as to ascertain why this quail was not eating. Meanwhile, this quail saw a moment's inattention on the part of the quail hunter, and he flew away to the forest.

When he went home, his relatives surrounded him and asked, "What happened to you? Why were you away for such a long time?" He said that he had been captured by a hunter, and related how he had obtained his release.

Buddha said, comparing the two stories, "Wise people are released from death as this quail. The quail at that time was I who have attained Buddhahood, the master who became the teacher of the three worlds."

The moral: "Parents love children."
Further,
"The practice of common sense is essential for a safe life."

119

The Story of the Rooster That Crows at the Wrong Time

(*Akālarāvi-Jātaka*)

Once when the Buddha was living in Jetavana monastery, there were two monks who did not do their monastic duties at the proper times. They would go to bed late at night, and they did not wake up at the proper time. When they woke up, they made a lot of noise. Because of this, the monks who slept normal hours nearby could not get sound sleep.

This story was spread among the monks who assembled for the evening Dhamma sermon of the Buddha in the preaching hall. The Buddha went in the evening to preach and asked, "Oh monks, what was your discussion before I came here?" The monks said, "Venerable sir, such-and-such monks shout and make noise at improper times during the night. We were discussing that." Buddha said, "Oh monks, it is not only today but also in the past that these two monks have been noisy at improper times." Buddha was then invited to disclose the story of the past. He delivered this story to disclose the previous life:

When Brahmadatta was ruling in Benares in the past, the Enlightenment Being was born in a notable Brahmin family. He was well educated, became the chief instructor in the area, and taught 500 students.

The students had a certain rooster who crowed at the proper times. They woke up at the proper time each day, and studied every morning learning their lessons by heart.

Then the rooster died.

After that, one student went to the forest to collect firewood. There he caught a wild rooster. He put it in a cage, and fed it regularly.

That rooster did not crow at the proper times. Sometimes, he would crow at midnight. Hearing the noise of the rooster, the students would get up at midnight and read their lessons so as to learn them by heart. But as it was too early to wake up, they became very upset. Sometimes, this rooster would crow in the middle of the morning. When they got up at that time, they did not have enough time to do their studies during the morning hours. So the rooster became very unpopular among the students. They killed it and complained to the teacher.

The teacher said, "Without teachers and parents, and without proper instruction, this fowl came to such a fate. Therefore, students must follow the guidance of teachers."

Buddha then compared these two incidents, and finished this story disclosing, "The fowl that crowed at the improper time was one of these monks who has no set time for his work. The students were you who are assembled here. The teacher was I, the Buddha, who attained Nibbāna."

The moral: "Learn to work at proper times."

120

The Story of Being Released from Bondage
(*Bandhanamokkha-Jātaka*)

When the Buddha was living in the Jeta Grove, the Buddha related this story regarding the Brahmin girl Ciñcā. Its present story is explained in the *Mahāpaduma-Jātaka* in the twelfth book [No. 472].

[After the Buddha's attainment of enlightenment, the Jains and other ascetics found that their gains had fallen. Therefore, the Jain recluses became upset and angry, and they hatched a conspiracy to defame the Buddha. Ciñcā, the Brahmin girl, became their instrument. In accord with the conspiracy, she came from home toward the Jetavana monastery every evening wearing a red cloth. Then she slept at a recluse's home, and returned to her home each morning as if she were a person coming from Jetavana monastery. People asked, "Where did you go?" She answered, "Do not care about where I go. Do not think about me." And she behaved so as to create doubts in people's minds about her.

She continued in this fashion for four months. By doing this, she led people to believe that she was no doubt coming from the Buddha's chamber. She used to say, "Now I am one month pregnant." "Now I am two months pregnant." "Now I am three months pregnant." And so forth. When ten months had passed like this, she pretended to be a woman who was about to deliver a baby.[7] Then she went to the Buddha having stuffed something around her belly, and when Buddha was preaching, in the middle of the congregation she accused the Buddha, saying, "Ah, you are preaching here as if a person who is innocent. I am now ten months

---

7 The months here are lunar months. Lunar months are shorter than our Western solar months. Hence, there are ten months of pregnancy instead of nine.

pregnant and I have to deliver my baby. I have no home in which to deliver. Why do you not prepare the food and other items that I need for my delivery of the baby? Mention it to King Kosala or to millionaire Anāthapiṇḍika and arrange someplace for me to stay."

The Buddha said, "Oh sister, the truth of this incident is known by both of us. Except for the two of us, who will know the truth?" At the same moment, there came four deities as rats. They scurried up her body, and cut the strings holding what was tied around her belly. The cloths that were tightened there fell down to the ground.

Everyone started to censure her. People attacked her because she had falsely accused the Buddha. And they kicked her out of the hall. Suddenly there came a big fire from hell (*Avici*), and the ground opened and took her.]

Regarding this, there was then discussion in the preaching hall. The Buddha revealed the story of the past thus:

Once the Enlightenment Being was born as a Brahmin advisor to King Brahmadatta, who ruled in Benares. He had a very beautiful queen who loved him very much. Because the king loved her so much, he once said to her, "For whatever you desire, you may ask." The queen responded, "I have everything I want. I have nothing to ask. And so, I ask you not to look at any other woman with passion. That is my boon." The king said, "Since there are 16,000 beautiful women in my possession, I may not be able to give that boon." She then pleaded, again and again. Very ardently, she continued to so plead. Finally, the king was unable to say "no" to her, and agreed.

While they were living in such a manner, deeply in love with one another, there was a riot in a remote village. His minister could not settle it. Finally, the king went there with his fourfold army. Before he left, he summoned his queen and said, "War is doubtful. It is difficult to bring women to the battlefield. One cannot retreat quickly with women beside you. Therefore, I cannot take you to the battlefield. Stay at home." The queen said, "No. Let me come with you." But the king was steadfast.

Then the queen said, "If such be so, please inform me of all news every Yojana."[8] The king and queen both agreed to this. And the king left, asking his ministers to look after the queen. The chief Brahmin advisor undertook her protection within the confines of the city. Every Yojana the king sent a messenger to inform her of his affairs, and to inquire about her well-being.

When each messenger came, the queen asked, "Why did you come?" Each messenger replied, "I came to inquire about your safety and happiness." Thereupon the queen summoned each to her chamber, was intimate with each of them, and then sent each back. Meanwhile, on the battlefield, the king won. During his thirty-two Yojana long trip, the queen was intimate with thirty-two messengers. Coming back, he also sent thirty-two messengers, and each of these was also intimate with the queen. The queen in this way was intimate with sixty-four messengers.

Finally, the king came near the city and camped overnight. He informed the chief Brahmin advisor the news of his arrival. The chief advisor decorated the city to welcome the king and his army. And he went to the palace to inform the queen of the king's arrival. The queen, seeing the beauty of his body, said, "Come and sit on the bed." The advisor, who was the Enlightenment Being, said, "Your majesty, the king who is your husband is handsome. I am both afraid of him, and of what might befall me in my next birth." When she heard this, she said, "Were not those sixty-four messengers who came to me also afraid of the king the same as you are? And were they also not afraid of their next birth?" Then the advisor said, "Even though I have reached my present age, I have never seen a woman with such a lustful mind. Therefore, please do not speak to me in this way." She said, "If you say 'no' to me, then I will ask the king to behead you complaining that you have asked me to be intimate with you." The advisor, who was the Enlightenment Being, said, "Not only in one life, but also in a thousand lives, even if you have me beheaded, I will not agree to your desires." Saying so, he left.

8 1 Yojana = roughly 7 miles.

The queen got angry. She scratched her body everywhere, and applied oil to the wounds. Wearing a dirty garment, she lay in her bedroom. She told her servant girls that when the king comes and asks about her, to tell him that she was sick and was lying in her bed.

The Enlightenment Being went forward to welcome the king and his army, who returned to the city triumphantly with a very big procession. The king came into the palace after circumambulating the city and not seeing the queen in the palace, he asked the servant girls about her. They said she was sick. Then the king went into her sleeping room and saw that she was lying in bed. Touching her back, he asked how she was feeling. After asking her two or three times, she turned around toward him and replied, "Ah, your lordship also has come. Now I am with my husband." Hearing these words, the king asked, "Why do you speak so?" Then she complained about the advisor, saying, "He did what no husband would ask him to do." And she showed her bruises to the king. The king got very angry, and ordered his security people to handcuff the Brahmin advisor and to kill him.

The security people, hearing these words, took the Brahmin advisor and brought him to the place of execution beating the death drums. Then the Enlightenment Being thought, "This happened because of the queen. But I must use my common sense here." Thinking so, he said to the executioners, "I know many places where wealth is hidden. Please do not kill me until I show them to the king." Then they asked, "What can you show the king?" The advisor said, "Because of me, the king has much wealth hidden. If you kill me, he will lose all this wealth not knowing where it is. Therefore, my death will be a big loss for him." The executioners heard this, and thought, "He says the truth." So they took him back to the king.

On seeing him, the king asked, "You, Brahmin, without having fear or shame did such a bad deed. Why did you do it?" The Enlightenment Being said, "Your lordship, I never did such a thing. From the earliest time I can remember, I have never even killed a louse. I have never even taken so much as a piece of grass that was not given. I have never looked at another's woman with lustful thoughts, and have never looked at another's woman with head raised.[9] Even in jest, I have never said falsehoods. I have never tasted alcohol, even as little as would be on a blade of grass. The sixty-four messengers are the people who misbehaved with the queen. Even though she trapped me in the same way, I did not get involved. That is why she complained about me."

On hearing this, the king summoned all the sixty-four messengers and also the queen. He questioned them as to whether or not this was true. They all admitted to their wrongdoing. The king ordered all of them to be killed. But the Enlightenment Being said, "Your lordship, these people did what the queen requested. Therefore, it is not right to punish them." And they were saved from punishment, and were retained in their positions. And he said further, "This is the nature of women. Therefore, it would be correct to excuse the queen as well." He in this way saved her also.

Finally he thought, "All this happened to me as I was in the life of a householder. Therefore, it would be good to renounce lay life." Thinking so, while his relatives cried, giving up all his wealth behind him, he went to the Himalayan forest and became ordained as an ascetic. After meditating there, he generated the fivefold higher knowledge and the eightfold high achievements of concentration. After his death, he was born in the Brahma world.

Buddha said, "The queen at that time was Ciñcā. The king was the Venerable Ānanda. And the advisor Brahmin was myself, the Buddha." And in this way he ended the story of release from bondage [*bandhanamokkha*].

The moral: "Truth always conquers."

9 It is polite to keep one's head lowered in the presence of another's wife.

121

The Story Regarding a Blade of Kusa Grass
(*Kusanāḷi-Jātaka*)

The Buddha delivered this story about Anāthapiṇḍika's true friend when he was in the Jetavanārāma of Anāthapiṇḍika in Sāvatthi. The millionaire Anāthapiṇḍika had a friend and he helped him as stated earlier in the *Kālakaṇṇi-Jātaka* [No. 83].

At one time there was a king called Brahmadatta in Benares. At that time the Enlightenment Being lived in the pleasure garden of the king and was a friend of the deity who possessed that park and who lived in the most prominent Sāla tree in the park. The Enlightenment Being lived in a clump of Kusa grass.

The king of Benares lived in a palace that had only one pillar supporting it. One day this pillar was shaken by the wind. The king decided to further support it. He summoned his carpenter and asked him to cut down any good tree with a core from the pleasure garden. The chief carpenter went to the pleasure garden, looked for an appropriate tree to cut down, and not seeing one decided finally with his assistant to cut down the prominent Sāla tree in the garden. He went back to the palace and reported about the problem, and about the prominent tree to the king.

The king said, "Even if it is the prominent tree, you cut it and repair the palace." Then the carpenter went with his assistant to cut down the tree. They made an appropriate reverence [*pūjā*], asking the deity who possessed the tree to move away from the tree. Hearing this request, the deity thought, "I do not have any other tree this large in the pleasure garden in which to stay." He began to cry, and his children also began to cry while they all embraced one another. All the other deities who were visiting there also started to cry. The deity who resided in the clump of Kusa grass also came upon hearing all this crying. He asked the reason for the crying. On hearing the reason, he said, "Please, do not be afraid. I know a way to save the tree." The next day, when the carpenters came to cut the tree, he made himself into a chameleon. He went through the roots of the tree, came up the tree on the far side so that people could not see him, and went to a top branch of the tree.

On seeing the chameleon on the top branches of the tree, the carpenter and his assistant thought, "This tree is hollow inside." They gave up the idea of cutting down the tree because it had no core inside.

Then the tree deity summoned the other deities and said, "Even though I was the highest deity in the pleasure garden, I did not know how to save my tree and palace. The deity who lived in a clump of Kusa grass understood how to protect it with his wisdom. Therefore, we must always associate with wise people, and not with the unwise." In this way, he preached to his fellow deities, and he became friendlier with the deity who possessed the clump of Kusa grass. Later, he passed away.

The pleasure garden deity was the Venerable Ānanda at that time. And I was born as the deity of the clump of Kusa grass.

And in this way, the Buddha finalized the Kusanāḷi story.

The moral: "Associate with the wise no matter what their station, not the unwise."

122

The Story of an Unwise Person
(*Dummedha-Jātaka*)

When the Buddha was living in the Bamboo Grove temple, once those monks who were assembled in the preaching hall were talking about the monk Devadatta. They said to each other, "Brothers, monk Devadatta even when seeing the Buddha's physical beauties, such as the thirty-two great marks of a great person [*mahāpurisa*] and the eighty additional attributes, a fathom wide halo, and physical beauties of the like, does not respect the Buddha and affords him no loving kindness. He has become jealous by thinking, 'I do not have such physical beauty.' And he wants to kill the Buddha."

Then the Buddha came there and sat on his seat. He asked, "Oh monks, what were you discussing before I came?" The monks replied, "Your reverence, we were talking about the monk Devadatta's jealousy of the Buddha." The Buddha said, "Monks, it is not only now, but even in the past he was jealous of me." The monks said, "Please, sir, disclose that story to us." The Buddha, after that invitation, stated the following story:

Long ago in ancient days, there was a king called Magadha in the city of Rājagaha. The Enlightenment Being was born among elephants, was white, and was very beautiful. He was in service to King Magadha.

Once, King Magadha got onto this white elephant that was well caparisoned and left in a grand procession to go to the city. The citizens, on seeing this elephant's beautiful body that was well shaped and large, said, "Oh, what a nice elephant. Such a big elephant is good for a universal monarch, and not for a king like this." Talking so, the people appreciated only the elephant, and not the king. On hearing such appreciation of the elephant, the king got angry, thinking, "These people did not appreciate me, who is their king." He became in this way jealous of the elephant, and thought of killing him. Thinking so, he summoned the mahout and said, "I want to know whether you trained this royal elephant to be obedient. If so, I want to examine it. Climb with him to the top of Vephulla Mountain." The mahout did so. And the king followed him with his ministers. He ordered the mahout to lead the elephant to a precipice. The mahout did so. The king then asked the mahout to have the elephant stand on three feet. He did so. Then the king ordered to have the elephant hold up its front two feet. He did so. Then the king asked him to have the elephant raise up its hind legs. He did so. Then he asked the mahout to have the elephant stand on one foot. He did so. And the elephant still did not fall. Then the king said, "Ask the elephant to go forward toward the precipice raising all four legs into the air."

The mahout thought, "This king wants to kill the elephant. This is just a stratagem." He said secretly to his elephant, "Your lordship, he is trying to kill you. If you can, get up into the sky and flee away to the city of Benares." At that very same moment, there arose a certain miraculous power on account of the virtue from previous merit, and miraculously the elephant jumped up into the sky. Then the mahout said to the king, "Your lordship, this elephant is not appropriate for such a person as you who has so little merit. Therefore, this elephant is not fit for such a foolish king as you. You stay there by yourself." And he had the elephant go through the sky to Benares to the king's palace grounds. People saw this, and they were surprised and became very happy. They ran to the king and informed him about this. The king came to that place and saw the elephant. And he said with great pleasure, "If this elephant will allow me to mount it, I request you to come down to the ground." And the elephant came down to the ground.

The mahout got down from the elephant and gave respect to the king. The king asked, "Why, son, did you come with this elephant?" The mahout told him everything. The king thanked him, saying, "You have done a good deed." Being satisfied, the king took the elephant into his possession. He divided Benares into three parts. He gave one part to the elephant, the second part to the mahout, and the third part he kept for himself. And he ruled righteously. Finally, he passed away according to his Kamma.

The Buddha, finalizing the story, said, "The king of Benares at that time was the Venerable Sāriputta. The mahout was the Venerable Ānanda. And King Magadha was the monk Devadatta. I, who am now the Buddha, was the elephant." Saying so, the Buddha ended this Jātaka story of an unwise person.

The moral: "While lack of wisdom brings death, wisdom brings happiness."

123

The Story of a Plough Handle
(*Naṅgalīsa-Jātaka*)

Once while the Buddha was living in Jetavana monastery, this story was delivered about Venerable Kāḷudāyi. He used to go to preach to gatherings. As he often could not understand the purpose of the gatherings, sometimes he would preach sad things to a happy community and happy things to a grieving community. As he could not preach appropriately to communities, he obtained a bad name. The community of monks knew this. One time, the monks who were assembled in the hall of law for the evening preaching were talking about this matter.

When the Buddha came there, he asked, "Oh monks, what were you talking about before I arrived?" The monks said, "Your lordship, we were talking about the lack of understanding of Venerable Kāḷudāyi in preaching." Then the Buddha said, "Monks, Kāḷudāyi not only acts like this today. Even in the past, he has acted in the same way." And Buddha was invited to disclose the story of the past that had been hidden by the course of time. Buddha preached the story of the past.

This is how it was:

Long ago in the past, there was a king called Brahmadatta in Benares. At that time, the Enlightenment Being was a prominent teacher in the city. He lived by giving instruction to students. People who were rich enough to afford it gave a thousand gold coins to the teacher. Some, who had not much money, got their education by working as servants to the master. And in this way, they were able to study.

Once there came a poor foolish man to get an education from the Enlightenment Being. He was paying for his education by working. One day he was massaging his master's feet, and the master requested that he raise up his feet. The student agreed, and under one side of the foot of the bed he placed folded cloth. As he had nothing for the other side, he placed his thigh under the bed. All that night, until the next morning, he kept his thigh under the bed forgoing his rest. In the morning, when the master awoke, he saw that the student was sitting at his foot, and he became very sad. He thought, "This poor foolish man works here as a slave, and cannot learn anything. Therefore, it would be good to somehow teach this man something." Thinking so, he said to the foolish student, "Whatever you see daily, you must tell me. And also relate to me a comparable thing [*upamā*]." The Enlightenment Being thought that by the student making a comparison, he would be able to develop his thinking.

The next day, the teacher asked the student to bring some firewood. When the student returned, the master requested, "Tell me whatever you have seen." The student said, "I have seen a snake in the forest." The master asked, "What did the snake resemble?" The student responded, "The snake was like a plough handle." The master thought, "A snake is long, and a plough handle is also long. Therefore his example is correct." Thinking so, he was satisfied.

The following day, he also went to the forest to bring firewood. And on that day, he saw an elephant. On returning, he said to his master that he had seen an elephant. The master asked him for a comparison. The student said, "It is like a plough handle." The teacher thought, "The end of an elephant's trunk is similar to a snake's head. Therefore it is a good comparison." And he was satisfied.

On still the next day, he went again into the forest. There he saw sugarcane. When he returned, he told his master, "I have seen sugarcane." The master again asked for a comparison. He said, "It is like a plough handle." The master thought, "Sugarcane is long, and the trunk of an elephant is also long. Therefore the comparison is correct." And he was satisfied.

The next day, when he went to the place where lunch was to be given, he ate curd and rice. After eating the curd and rice, he returned.

He told his master, "I have eaten curd and rice." His master asked for a similar thing to curd and rice. He said, "It is like a plough handle."

The teacher had been satisfied with the previous three answers. But in this case he thought, "What a foolish man this is. No matter how hard I try, I will not be able to make him a wise man." And he gave up his efforts to make the student a person with understanding.

The foolish student at that time is today Kāḷudāyi. I who am the Buddha was his master at that time.

Saying so, he completed the discourse of the Jātaka story.

The moral: "Even if good luck is in an unwise man's pocket, he will lose it."

124

The Story of Water
(*Amba-Jātaka*)

At one time, Buddha was living in Jetavana monastery. Once there came to that place a young man, and the Buddha ordained him. From the day that he was ordained, he was very strict in performing his duties properly. He did all duties such as sweeping the compound, the preaching hall, and the temple complex, as well as bringing water for washing and drinking, all at their proper times without being lazy. Due to his tireless work, all the lay people were very happy. They gave 500 bowls of water daily, and that water was very useful to many hundreds of monks. This story went mouth to mouth among the monks, and finally it reached the hall of law where Buddha preached in the evening. When this was being discussed there, Buddha went early to the preaching hall and asked them, "Oh monks, what were you talking about before I came?" They said, "Venerable Bhante, because of the newly ordained young monk, we are becoming the beneficiaries of many things. We were talking about that." The Buddha said, "Oh monks, not only today has this monk been beneficial to us because of his dutifulness and punctuality, but also he was so in the past." Then the monks requested the Buddha to disclose this monk's past.

This is how the former story was:

Long ago, a king called Brahmadatta was ruling in Benares. At that time, the Enlightenment Being was born in a well-known Brahmin family. But by seeing the disadvantages of sensual desires, he renounced his lay life and went to the Himalayan forest, joining 500 ascetics. He became their chief.

At that time in the Himalayan forest, there was a severe drought. There was no rain for a long time. As the ponds and lakes dried up and wild animals had no water to drink, they suffered a lot. One out of the 500 ascetics cut down a tree and hollowed out a trough in which to keep water. Daily he put water from a well in this trough, constantly replenishing it. The wild animals became very happy by his efforts. They understood that because of this he had no time to go to fetch fruit for his meal. Therefore they discussed this with each other, and determined that when each came to take water, each would bring some fruit like mangoes, jackfruit, and such other edible fruit. When this happened, there became a large quantity of fruit to be eaten by the 500 ascetics.

The Enlightenment Being understood this situation and said to the ascetics, "We 500 obtained these sweet edible fruit without having to go into the forest because of this one ascetic who made such an effort to give water to animals. Therefore, whether you are clergy or a lay person, everyone must make an effort to do good."

The ascetic, who fetched water from a well with much effort at that time, is today this dutiful monk. The leader of those ascetics at that time was myself who has become the Buddha.

The moral: "Be generous regardless of position or status."

125

The Story of Kaṭāhaka [One Who is an Empty Cauldron] (*Kaṭāhaka-Jātaka*)

This story was told regarding a monk who was boastful and who had a cunning mind. The story of that monk was given in the *Vikantana-Jātaka* (?).

At one time when Brahmadatta was ruling in Benares, the Enlightenment Being was born as a millionaire in that city. At that time a son was born to the Enlightenment Being in his house. On the very same day, a certain servant girl also gave birth to a child. The millionaire's son and the slave girl's son both grew up together. When the millionaire's son went to study, the servant girl's son also went there and learned how to write, how to count, and all the other subjects. He was known as Kaṭāhaka. He was very smart in commerce; also he was skilled in talking and debating. Therefore, the millionaire appointed him to look after his treasure.

One day the lad Kaṭāhaka thought, "This status will not be permanent to me forever. Whenever my employer sees a fault in me, he will brand my chest and put me back into slavery. Then I will have to suffer a lot." Therefore he thought, "Let me do a stratagem so I can remain in this status forever. Let me be friendly with the millionaire so as to gain his complete trust. He has another millionaire friend in a remote village. After being friendly with the millionaire, I will go to his millionaire friend and pretend to be the son of the millionaire. Doing so, I will marry his daughter and have her cook me food. If I do this, I will never lose the status I now have."

Thinking so, he wrote a letter to the millionaire in the remote village as if he were the millionaire himself introducing his son. This stated, "I send to you my son known as Kaṭāhaka for the purpose of marrying your daughter as our families are of the same caste and are appropriately matched to each other. Therefore please give your daughter to him, and he will be able to look after your wealth and so forth until I come to celebrate the marriage. I am at the moment unable to come as I have many things to do here. I will come later." Stating these things, he wrote such a letter. And he affixed to it the seal of the millionaire. As he was able to go anywhere in the millionaire's house, he stole some sandals, perfumes and comfortable clothes to give to the millionaire and his daughter, and he went to the millionaire's home in the remote village and paid his respects to him.

Then the millionaire asked, "From where did you come?" And he said, "I came from Benares." The millionaire asked, "Whose son are you?" And he said, "I am the son of the millionaire of Benares." Then he asked, "Why did you come here?" And he took out the letter he had brought, and giving it to the millionaire he said, "You can understand why I came here by reading this."

The millionaire read the letter and became very happy. And he gave him for marriage to his daughter together with great wealth and many luxurious things.

After that, when the millionaire's daughter was using those luxurious things that were supposedly sent by the millionaire of Benares, Kaṭāhaka used to humiliate her saying, "Did you ever have these types of things before—such perfumes, sweets and so forth, as these?" And when he was given rice and such other things to eat, he would say, "I cannot eat this type of rice and food. It is the poor fare of the provinces." And when he was given perfume and flowers, he would say, "I cannot use these village products." He always used to belittle her, saying that he was from the city and she was from the country.

When the millionaire of Benares found that his slave was gone, he wanted to get him back. Later, he heard that his slave Kaṭāhaka was living in the country millionaire's village. Hearing this, the millionaire decided to visit the country millionaire and he got permission from the king to go there. This was heard here and there, and in due course Kaṭāhaka also heard this news. Kaṭāhaka thought, "There is no doubt that he is coming to get me and to hurt me as I have done this deception." And he thought further, "It would not be good to hide. It would be better to stay here, and when he comes I will work for him as I have done previously. In this way, I will win his mind. Then I can live freely." Thinking this, he let it be known to everyone, "We city people are not like you provincials. When we see our parents, we live with the fear and shame of doing bad deeds. We do not sit together with them, and do not eat together with them. We wash our parents' feet, take them water for bathing, and do all such necessary things as if we were their servants." Meanwhile, the millionaire came to a nearby village and stayed there.

Hearing this, Kaṭāhaka went to his father-in-law and said, "Father-in-law, our father will come to this village soon. It would be good to make arrangements to welcome him and to organize hospitality for when he arrives." And the country millionaire did so.

When the Benares millionaire came, he was very much welcomed. And after he was well entertained, after their lunch, the Benares millionaire went to take a rest. Then Kaṭāhaka took a container of water and placed it near the Benares millionaire's bed, and kneeling down paid obeisance to the Benares millionaire. He begged him, "Your lordship, whatever you want me to do, I will do for you. But please, do one thing for me. Please do not destroy my present situation here, and do not reveal me." The millionaire on seeing his humble nature and obedience, and his unconceited air, said, "Do not worry about that. I will not reveal you and put you down from your position."

When the two millionaires were chatting, the country millionaire said, "Sir, when you sent your son I did everything for him, and I also gave my daughter to him. I did not omit doing anything for him." The Benares millionaire said, "That is a very good thing that you have done. Our friendship has developed into a relationship now." And he stayed there for a few days enjoying his hospitality.

One day, the Benares millionaire's supposed daughter-in-law was combing his hair, and he asked her, "How is your husband? Are you happy with him or not? Do you get along, or does he put on airs with you?" She said, "Your lordship, he is not bad with others. But he has one weakness. When I do something wrong, he abuses me saying that I am a dirty woman. But there is nothing more."

Then the millionaire said, "I will teach you a verse to tell him if he says this again." Teaching her that, after a few days he left for Benares.

Kaṭāhaka was with him, and left with him as far as the next village. He did not let anyone else talk with him. He said, "goodbye," after going a certain distance, and then came back. [He then became even more conceited than before, as nothing bad had happened against him.]

One day, his wife prepared rice for his lunch, and on seeing this rice he said, "This is the rice you give to me? This is village rice. It cannot be eaten by city people." Then the millionaire's daughter recited the Pāli verse that was taught by the millionaire of Benares:

"One speaks boastfully when he goes to a remote village.

"Without saying unnecessary things, Kaṭāhaka, eat this rice."

She did not know the meaning of this stanza, since she was not well educated. Kaṭāhaka, though, understood it, and he became afraid. From that point on, Kaṭāhaka did not complain too much.

The real meaning of this stanza is this:

"Kaṭāhaka, just because you come from another part of this country to here, do not put down everything and everyone. Why do you not mind your former status? Your millionaire lordship this time returned without doing anything. If he comes back, the next time he will put a branding on your chest and take you back."

Saying so, the Buddha ended the story and further said, "This monk was the boastful Kaṭāhaka at that time. The millionaire of Benares was I who am the Buddha."

The moral: "Being cunning will not gain all things."

126

The Story of the Characteristics of Swords
(*Asilakkhaṇa-Jātaka*)

At one time Buddha was living in Jetavanārāma. At that time the king of Kosala had a Brahmin who could tell whether a sword was lucky by smelling it. When smiths would bring their swords, if they had given bribes, he said, "It is good." To those who did not give bribes, he said to them, "It is bad." All in the course of time knew the deceptive nature of this man. Knowing his nature, one smith made a sword and making it very sharp, put it in a sheath filled with hot chili powder. He brought it to the king. The king summoned the Brahmin and requested him to tell them the goodness or badness of the sword.

The Brahmin, in accord with the order of the king, took the sword out from the sheath and placing it near his nose tried to smell it. Immediately, before he could say anything, the chili powder smelled by him caused him to sneeze. He could not remove the sword from his nose quickly enough, so when he sneezed, the sword cut off the tip of his nose. This story spread everywhere and eventually it reached even the monks in the preaching hall.

One day in the preaching hall of Jetavanārāma the assembled monks were speaking about this. When the Buddha visited there, the monks paid respect to the Buddha. The Buddha asked, "Oh monks, what were you discussing before I came here?" Then the monks related the story of the Brahmin who smelled swords for the king of Kosala. Buddha said, "Not only today this man faced this mishap, but also in the past he faced the same fate." The monks requested the Buddha to disclose the past story. The Buddha spoke then the past story:

At one time, a king called Brahmadatta ruled in Benares. He had a fortune-telling Brahmin who by smelling swords could tell their goodness or badness. He took bribes from the sword smiths. He condemned the work of those smiths who had not given bribes because they had not given him bribes.

Once a certain trickster smith made a good sword and made it well sharpened. He applied hot chili powder to it and took it to the king. The king summoned the Brahmin to examine the sword. As it was covered with hot chili powder, when he smelled it he sneezed before he was able to remove the sword from his nose. The tip of his nose was cut off, and he was ashamed because of this. The king became very sad because of this, and requested his craftsmen to make a fake tip for the Brahmin's nose with wax. And the Brahmin again asked to work for the king.

At this time the king had a nephew at his palace, and also his daughter. The two of them since they were very young, had grown up together. When they got older, they fell in love with each other. The king did not know this secret love. The king and his ministers one day discussed the marriage of the princess. The king said, "I will give my daughter to a prince of another kingdom. If I do so, I will gain two new supporters, the prince and his father, to defend my kingdom." Since then, the princess was not allowed to see the nephew with whom she had grown up so as to try to prevent them from falling in love. This strengthened their love for one another. And the nephew wanted to marry the princess as they both were now grown up.

The nephew therefore made a stratagem to marry the princess. He met the servant woman of the princess and gave her a bribe of a thousand gold coins. He requested her to keep the princess away for one day from the palace so that he could get to her. The woman said, "Do not worry. I will do it. I will take responsibility for that."

Thinking of a stratagem, she went to the king and said, "Your lordship, your daughter is under the influence of an evil spirit. She is becoming unlucky and emaciated. Therefore, we will have to remove the evil spirit from her body." The king asked, "What can we do for that?" The woman said, "In such-and-such a place there is a certain cemetery. There you need to make a stage. Keep a corpse on top of it, and cover it placing a bed over the dead body. We will place the princess on the bed and bathe her. Then the evil spirit will leave her."

Hearing this, the king ordered her to do all these things and gave her all she had requested. She then undertook the task. She also tied some dried chili powder in a cloth, and she hid it near the bed so the nephew would be able to take it. She requested the nephew to go there and lie under the bed as the dead body. She explained to the nephew how to carry this off. The woman said to the caretakers, "When I come to the cemetery and wash the princess, the dead body will sneeze two or three times, come out from under the bed, and seize and devour the first one whom he sees. Therefore, be warned. Run away." This was also mentioned to the nephew and princess, and the nephew was told, "When the caretakers run away, take the princess out of the cemetery, and after taking a bath with her go wherever you like."

On the day they set to have the service, the nephew went early and lay down under the bed she had prepared. The woman mentioned again to all the caretakers in the cemetery, "When the dead body sneezes, you will have to be ready for the death of the first one he seizes." When, as she said, the nephew started to sneeze, all the caretakers laying their weapons down beside them, ran away from the cemetery screaming loudly. The retinue and other dignitaries who had come to witness this also all ran away.

When the nephew came out from under the bed, he took the princess, took a good bath, and went to his house with her. Hearing this news, the king became happy and he gave his daughter to the nephew.

Finalizing this story the Buddha said, "At that time the fortune-telling Brahmin who was skilled in sniffing swords was this fortune-telling Brahmin of today. The nephew prince of the king of Benares was I who am the Buddha."

The moral: "What causes a loss for one person, may cause a gain for someone else."

127

The Story of Kalaṇḍuka
(*Kalaṇḍuka-Jātaka*)

At one time Buddha was living in Jetavanārāma and delivered this story of Kalaṇḍuka on a certain occasion because of a boastful monk. This monk was boastful as was the monk in the story of the present regarding Kaṭāhaka [No. 125].

Just as its present story is similar to the story of Kaṭāhaka, so here also in the same way our Kalaṇḍuka studied as a young boy with the son of the millionaire of Benares. The reader will have to understand that Kalaṇḍuka also acted in the very same capacity in the millionaire's palace looking after the property of the millionaire of Benares. He as well wrote a bogus letter to the millionaire of a remote village introducing himself as the son of the Benares millionaire, and signed it with the millionaire's signet ring. All other incidents are also similar to the aforementioned story of Kaṭāhaka.

The only difference in this story is that one day after living together with the daughter of the millionaire of the remote village, the boastful boy who married the young woman scorned her on one occasion when they went to take a bath together.

The story is as follows:

At one point the millionaire of Benares did not see Kalaṇḍuka in the palace for a period of time. As he did not see the young lad, he asked his parrot to find him. The parrot said, "Yes." And he left the palace to see where Kalaṇḍuka had gone. Luckily, he came to the place where Kalaṇḍuka and his wife had come to take a bath in the river. The parrot, on seeing him, hid in the middle of some branches of a rose apple tree so as to observe them. While Kalaṇḍuka was lying in the water, the millionaire's daughter, his wife, gave him a decoction of perfumed milk to drink. Kalaṇḍuka took the cup into his hands, rinsed his mouth with the perfumed milk and spit it out over her head. The parrot saw this. The parrot could not tolerate such an insult to a noble woman by the slave Kalaṇḍuka. He came out of his hiding place and said, "Hey, Kalaṇḍuka. Even though I am a forest bird, you and I both lived together in the palace. Do you not understand your position? Is it right to scorn such a noble woman by spitting over her head? The milk that you took into your mouth ought to have been drunk, not spit out."

Kalaṇḍuka heard this. [The millionaire's daughter also heard this.] Kalaṇḍuka thought, "If this parrot discloses my situation to others, it will not be good." Addressing the parrot, he said, "O honorable parrot, please come and talk to me. How are you?" Then the parrot, hearing these words, thought, "As I disclosed his position, there is no doubt that if I go to his hand and perch on it he will kill me, strangling me by the neck." Thinking so, he rose up to the sky and went back to Benares. He described what he had seen to the millionaire of Benares.

The millionaire of Benares, on hearing the story, decided to bring back Kalaṇḍuka to Benares as his slave.

The Buddha finalized the story saying, "Kalaṇḍuka at that time was the present boastful monk. And I who have become the Buddha was the millionaire of Benares."

The moral: "Do not overstep one's bounds, and respect the positions of others."

128

The Story of the Cat[10]
(*Biḷāra-Jātaka*)

At one time, Buddha was living in Jetavanārāma in Sāvatthi. While he was there, a certain cunning, deceptive and hypocritical monk was brought to his attention. Buddha, on seeing him, said, "Monks, this man is not only cunning, deceptive and hypocritical today. He also was so in the past." Then the monks requested the Buddha to disclose this monk's past. Buddha thus related his past story:

Long ago in ancient times, there was a king called Brahmadatta in Benares. While he was ruling Benares, the Enlightenment Being was born as a rat. He was wise, and his physical appearance was fat like that of a boar. Thousands of rats lived with him in a big anthill in the forest. They respected him as their leader.

Meanwhile, a certain jackal that was searching for prey, wandering here and there, saw this large group of rats. He thought, "By some sort of stratagem, I will be able to eat those rats." Thinking so, one day he stood on the path the Enlightenment Being was to travel on, with one foot raised, his mouth open, and facing the sun. The Enlightenment Being who was searching for food, on seeing him asked, "Who are you?" Then the jackal

10 Though the story here is about a jackal, the corresponding story in the *Mahābhārata* is about cat. See *Mahābhārata* 5.160.15-43 in the Bombay edition, *Mahābhārata* 5421-49 in the Calcutta edition. The corresponding passage is deleted from *Mahābhārata* 5.157 in the Critical Edition (Poona edition), but it is referred to in the critical apparatus for *Mahābhārata* 5.157.5d and 16, and is given in full in Appendix I, no. 9 (vol. 6, pp. 667b-669a). The story is not included in either Pratap Chandra Roy's translation of the *Mahābhārata* (1883-96; rpt. 1952-62), or in J. A. B. van Buitenen's uncompleted translation of the Critical Edition of the *Mahābhārata* (Books 1-5, 1973-78). The jackal in the story here acts like a cat.

said, "I am the righteous one." Then he asked, "Why are you standing on one leg?" He replied, "If I stand on all four legs, the earth would not bear my weight." Then he asked, "Why do you keep your mouth open?" He replied, "I am eating the wind." Then he asked, "Why are you facing east?" He replied, "I am worshipping the rising sun." Then the Enlightenment Being thought, "This jackal is not a liar. No doubt he is saying the truth. There is a wholesome quality in his heart." Thinking so, he came two times a day to respect him. He came attended by other rats. When they were returning, the jackal every time caught the last rat and ate it. He wiped away the blood on this mouth, and then stood as he had been doing.

After he had been engaged in this hypocrisy daily, the number of rats in the troop started to decline noticeably. On seeing their numbers decline, the other rats approached the Enlightenment Being and said, "Your lordship, long ago when we were inside the anthill, we were so crowded we kept touching each other. But now, our numbers are sparse. We do not know why this is so. Please be kind enough to explain the situation to us."

The Enlightenment Being, hearing the news, thought, "There is no doubt, this must be the doing of the jackal." And on that day, when he went with the other rats to pay respect to the jackal he stayed in the rear, sending all the other rats before him. When the jackal saw the Enlightenment Being in the rear, he jumped on him as he had done to the other rats previously. The Enlightenment Being jumped out of the way and was thus saved. He thought, "This jackal's penance is similar to the penance of a cat."[11] Thinking so, he came to the determination that the jackal's penance was only a deception to get his food. He jumped up onto the neck of the jackal and bit at his windpipe, and killed him.

---

11 A pretender to virtue is called "one who acts like a cat" according to the 'Laws of Manu' (*Mānavadharmaśāstra*) 4.195. Also, see the Tamil book of proverbs 'The Hand Which Holds the Spear of Victory' (*Veṟṟi Vēṟkai*) 42: "There is not for a cat either penance or compassion." A cat is a hypocrite.

Those rats that saw this incident came there and ate all the flesh of the jackal. The latecomers among those rats got little flesh. After that, those rats lived happily.

Thus the Buddha ended the story, disclosing that he, the Buddha, had been the king of the rats.

The moral: "It is difficult to deceive others every day."

(129)

The Story of the Jackal That Worshipped Fire
(*Aggika-Jātaka*)

When Buddha was living in Jetavanārāma in Sāvatthi, this story was delivered about a monk who knew many deceptions and trickeries:

Long ago in ancient times King Brahmadatta was ruling in Benares. At the time he was ruling, the Enlightenment Being was born as a rat. In the meantime, a certain jackal was burned by fire and only the hair on the top of his head remained. Then, the jackal whose hair on the top of his head had been preserved saw himself in a reflection. He thought, "How can I live now only with hair on the top of my head?" Seeing the Enlightenment Being and his retinue of rats, he thought, "There is now one way that I can live." Thinking so, he went to those rats and became friendly with them. As was mentioned in the previous Jātaka story, he paid obeisance to the Enlightenment Being and the Enlightenment Being asked, "Who are you?" He said, "I am Bharadvāja, Worshipper of Fire." The Enlightenment Being asked, "Why did you come here?" He said, "I came to look after you and your retinue." Then the Enlightenment Being again asked, "How can you protect us?" The jackal said, "When you go out in the morning for food, and come back in the evening, I will count your numbers and make sure as many return as left. That is how I can look after you." The Enlightenment Being said, "That is very good, uncle. Do so." Since then the jackal, as he pretended to count them in the morning and evening, would eat one of them each time they went and came back. Meanwhile, the rats began to notice that their ranks were dwindling.

The Enlightenment Being heard this and the next day he came out at the end of the pack. The jackal jumped up on the Enlightenment Being who was now last, as he had done previously on other rats. The

Enlightenment Being who had been mindful about this, jumped out of the way suddenly. He said, "Now I understand your promising to protect us. You have killed numbers of us. That is what you have done to us." Saying so, he jumped up onto the throat of the jackal and bit it, and killed him.

The jackal at that time was this hypocritical monk of today. And I was the king of rats, who has become the fully enlightened one today.

Saying so, the Buddha completed this story of the past.

The moral: "Hypocrisy will not serve one's ends for a long time."

130

The Story of a Lazy Person
(*Kosiya-Jātaka*)

When the Buddha was living in the monastery of Jeta Grove, one Brahmin who had become a follower of the Buddha had very pious feelings toward the Buddha, the law [*dhamma*] and the community of monks [*saṅgha*]. At that time, he had a wife who was living in his home, but as an adulterous woman. She would get up in the middle of the night and go out. During the daytime, without doing any work at home, she would recline on the bed and sleep.

The Brahmin would come home and ask, "Why are you sleeping?" The Brahmin woman would say, "I am sick." He asked, "What is the sickness?" She would say, "I have an upset stomach." The Brahmin asked, "What can I do for that?" She said, "I need sweet, delicious food." Because of that, the Brahmin daily would go out and beg alms for her. But, the sickness remained, without her recovering, for days on end. Therefore, the Brahmin thought of going to the Buddha to ask for a treatment for her. As he had not gone to see the Buddha for several days, he took some fragrances, flowers and lights in both hands, and went to the monastery. Paying his respects to the Buddha, he sat by his side.

Lord Buddha saw the Brahmin and asked, "You have not come to see me for so long. Why so?" The Brahmin said, "Your lordship, my wife was suffering with pain, and I was searching for treatment for her and so could not come. That is why I was away." And he continued his explanation, "Sir, even though she is sick for days, she is not weak, not lean or thin, and not of bad complexion. I have been giving her nourishing food as much as I can. Yet she does not seem to get well. Now I do not know what to do."

Then the Buddha said, "Because it is covered by re-births in the ocean of existence, you cannot understand it. Even in the past, I was the person who prescribed medicine for this sickness of hers." Then the Brahmin requested the Buddha to disclose the past.

The Buddha said the past story thus:

At one time when King Brahmadatta was reigning in Benares, the Enlightenment Being was born as the head teacher of the princes of a hundred and one cities. He taught both princes and Brahmin youths. One Brahmin learned completely the three Veda-s, writing, mathematics, logic, grammar, and the eighteen such subjects from the Enlightenment Being. This Brahmin would visit the teacher to serve him three times each day, and at the same time would clarify any doubts he had in his mind about the teachings. At the same time, the Brahmin's wife was unrighteous as mentioned in the above story. The disclosure of that situation was also similar to that mentioned in the above story.

The teacher said, "It is not necessary to give her nourishment and delicious foods. Instead of that, take cow's urine and boil in it five kinds of medicinal leaves, making a decoction. In that, place the three kinds of condiments and the three kinds of nuts [which are hard to swallow], making a decoction out of this. Put it in a copper pot and ferment it for several days so that it takes on the flavor of the copper. Then the smell becomes like cheese. Take that decoction to her, and taking with you a rope, creeper and bundle of sticks, tell her to drink this medicine to get rid of her sickness. Warn her, if she does not do so you will seize her by her hair and beat her with the rope, the creeper or the bundle of sticks. When you do so, she will recover from her sickness.

The Brahmin went home and did as the head teacher instructed. Then the woman asked, "Who prescribed this?" The Brahmin said, "This was told me by my master who has educated me." Then she understood there was no doubt that the teacher knew her behavior. She thought, "Why should I suffer drinking this distasteful decoction and undergoing other punishments?" She repented and determined to give up her bad behavior. She got up from her bed, and began to clean the house and do her other wifely duties.

Since then, she maintained her chastity and lived happily.

In the story of the present also, the pious Brahmin's wife heard that the Buddha asked about her sickness and she thought, "There is no doubt that the Buddha knows the unrighteousness that I have done." And she gave up her bad behavior as well.

"At that time, the Brahmin husband and wife were the same as today." And the Buddha said further, "I who am the Buddha today was born as the head teacher then."

The moral: "Truth will never be defeated by hypocrisy."

131

The Story of an Ill-Treated Gift
(*Asampadāna-Jātaka*)

When the Buddha was living in the Bamboo Grove monastery [Veḷuvanārāma] of Rājagaha this story was delivered one day to the monks who assembled in the preaching hall. They were talking about Devadatta's lack of gratitude.

The Buddha entered the preaching hall and asked, "Monks, what were you talking about before I came here?" They answered, "Your lordship, we were talking about Devadatta's ungrateful nature." Then the Buddha said, "Oh monks, not only today, but in ancient times as well he also was ungrateful." The monks requested the Buddha to disclose the past story. The Buddha disclosed the story as follows:

At one time there was a king called Magadha in the city of Rājagaha of the Magadha kingdom. The Enlightenment Being was born in the city to a wealthy family which had 800 million crores, and he was named Saṅkha the Millionaire.

At the same time, there was another very wealthy millionaire in Benares, known as Piliya. They were friends, and kept in contact with one another.

At one point, the millionaire Piliya of Benares went bankrupt. Being in such a situation, he thought, "It is now a good time to go to see my friend Saṅkha. I can perhaps get some wealth from him to help maintain my position." Thinking so, he left only with his wife. Leaving Benares on foot without even a vehicle, he came to the city of Rājagaha. He came to Saṅkha's palace, and appeared before Saṅkha. Saṅkha welcomed him and asked him the reason for his coming. Piliya said, "I have become bankrupt and there is no where for me to live now. That is why I came to see you."

The millionaire Saṅkha said, "It is very good that you have come. Do not worry." Saying so, he divided his wealth into two equal halves and gave Piliya 400 million crores from his wealth, together with servants and other necessities such as bullocks, cows, horses, elephants, chariots, and so forth. Treating him in this fashion, Saṅkha bade him to return home.

After a long time, Saṅkha fell into the same condition. "I am now suffering because of my downfall. There is, though, my good friend Piliya to whom I have given half of my wealth. Therefore, now it is time to go to see my friend Piliya. He will help me at this time." Thinking so, he went with his wife to Benares. He asked his wife to stay in an inn on the outskirts of the city while he went alone to see Piliya at Piliya's house. Piliya, hearing of Saṅkha's coming to his home, did not receive him well. When he came, he did not treat him with respect and did not even offer him a seat or chat with him in a friendly manner. He only asked the reason for his coming.

Saṅkha said, "I came to see you." Piliya then asked, "Where are you staying." Saṅkha said, "I have no place to stay." On that very same day, there had arrived at Piliya's home a thousand cartfuls of red rice. Not knowing the nature of gratitude, Piliya summoned a slave boy and said, "It is not good to send this man away empty handed. Therefore, measure him one measure of unhusked red rice and give it to this man." He said to the millionaire Saṅkha, "Take this, cook it, and eat it anywhere you like. Do not come back to see me again."

Hearing these words of Piliya, Saṅkha thought, "Do I take this or not?" Again he thought, "As I came here, it is not good to violate our friendship. Let whatever happens be. I will take it." And he took the measure of unhusked red rice and went back to where his wife was. On seeing this, his wife said, "You have given him 400 million crores. Why did you take this measure of rice?" He said, "If I did not take this, there is no doubt I would have violated our friendship. Therefore, I brought it so as not to violate our friendship. Do not worry." But Saṅkha's wife started to cry. Meanwhile, one of Saṅkha's former servants was passing nearby. He recognized the voices of the millionaire Saṅkha and of his wife who was crying. Recognizing them, he entered the inn and asked why Saṅkha's wife was crying. She said, "We have given Piliya 400 million crores of wealth together with retinue. But when we are having a hard time, this man has given us a measure of unhusked red rice." Then the former servant said, "Do not worry, your lordships. Come with me to my home." He took them to his home. And after giving them baths, he gave them food and entertained them very well. Introducing them to his friends, he requested them to honor Saṅkha and his wife. He went together with all of them to the royal palace, and made a clamor on account of this matter. Then the king of Benares, on hearing this noise, inquired as to its cause. He summoned both the millionaires of Rājagaha and of Benares and questioned them. Listening to them both, first he asked Saṅkha, "What did you give Piliya in his hard time?" Saṅkha said, "400 million crores of wealth." Then he asked Piliya, "Is it true?" Piliya said, "Yes." Then he asked, "When he came to you, what did you give?" Piliya remained silent. Then the king said, "I heard that you have given one measure of unhusked rice. Is it true?" Again, Piliya remained silent.

Then the king and his ministers censured Piliya. The king said to the millionaire Saṅkha, "You can take all of his wealth." The millionaire Saṅkha said, "Your majesty, I do not wish to take another's wealth. The 400 million crores that I have given him before is enough for me. I do not need another's wealth." So he took his wealth, and the people whom he had given to Piliya, and went to the city of Rājagaha. There in Rājagaha he put his affairs in order, and he did many meritorious deeds such as charity and so forth for the benefit of others. At the end of his life, he passed on happily.

At that time, Devadatta was Piliya. And I who have attained Buddhahood was the millionaire Saṅkha.

The moral: "Gratitude is noble."

132

The Story of Five Sensual Delights
(*Pañcagaru-Jātaka*)

When the Buddha was living in Jetavana monastery he delivered the discourse of *Ajapālanigrodha* [The Goatherd's Banyan Tree]. The monks one day got together in the preaching hall and said, "Brothers, the three daughters of Māra[12] were not able to tempt the Buddha when he was under the Bodhi tree.[13] They came to tempt the Buddha assuming beautiful bodies, and the Buddha did not even open his eyes to see them. He exercised great self-control." They lauded this behavior variously. While they were talking, Buddha came there and asked, "Monks, what were you talking about before I came?" The monks mentioned their discussion to the Buddha, and the Buddha said, "Monks, not only today, but even in the past I controlled my cravings for women. Therefore, there is no need to say that this is due to my enlightenment. When I, the Buddha, was not enlightened, even at such a time as the Enlightenment Being I was capable of self-control." Then the monks requested him to disclose the story of the past. The Buddha preached to them, disclosing the past story:

At one time when King Brahmadatta was ruling in Benares, he had 500 princes. The Enlightenment Being was born the last of them. He asked a solitary Buddha [*pacceka-buddha*] when he might become king of

---

12 The three daughters of Māra are Taṇhā, Arati, and Ragā.

13 See Palobhana Sutta, probably the Dhītaro Sutta of the Mārasaṃyutta, Saṃyuttanikāya (C. A. F. Rhys Davids and Sūriyagoḍa Sumaṅgala Thera, The Book of Kindred Sayings [Saṃyutta-Nikāya] or Grouped Suttas, Part I, Kindred Sayings with Verses [Sagāthā-Vagga], [1917]: 156-59 [IV, 3, §5]). See regarding this G. P. Malalasekhara, Dictionary of Pāli Proper Names, 1937-38: 2, 166 and 1, 1160-61.

the country. The Pacceka-Buddha answered, "If you can go to the city of Takkasilā, you can be the king within seven days."[14] On hearing this prediction of the Pacceka-Buddha, he took five ministers to help him and set forth to go there. On his way, all five ministers were tempted by a certain demoness and eaten by her. The demoness then chased after the Enlightenment Being, who came to the city of Gandhāra. While he was spending the night in a certain inn, the king of that city passed by riding on an elephant and saw the demoness. Seeing her beauty tempted the king. The Enlightenment Being, seeing the king with her, said, "Do not take her to your palace. She is a demoness." She said to the king, "No, no. I am his lordship's wife. He got angry with me, and that is why he is saying this." Believing her words, the king took her to his palace even after the Enlightenment Being had asked him not to do so. That same night, the demoness went back to her own home while the king was sleeping and came back to the palace with her attendants. They killed and ate everyone in the palace, including the king and queen, leaving behind only the bones. [This story was told previously in the *Gandhāra-Jātaka* (=*Telapatta-Jātaka*, Jātaka No. 96).]

When the demoness left, the next morning the officers who were living in the villages came back to the palace and as the doors were not opened for them, they broke down the doors and saw the bones of the king, the queen, and their retinue. They cleaned the whole palace, and decorated it as a palace in the divine world as it had been decorated before. It looked like the Sudhamma Hall of Sakka, the king of the gods. The officers summoned the ministers and discussed how to select a king. They finally came to the decision that they should invite the man who was in the inn and who warned the king not to take home the demoness. They went to him, and told him their decision. Then the Enlightenment Being said, "Does not the king have a son?" And the officers and ministers said, "No." Then he accepted the invitation, was anointed as the king,

---

14 Takkasilā was the capital of the kingdom of Gandhāra. In the Buddha's time, like Benares it was a center of learning.

and he came to the palace in a grand procession. After that, while he was sitting on the throne, he enjoyed the magnificence around him—his ministers, the officers, Brahmins, the commanders of the army, 16,000 dancing women, and others who were prominent in the kingdom, all dancing, playing music, beating drums, and singing. Because of these things, it was noisy like the roaring of a thunderstorm. They were playing the five-fold musical instruments, making the environment noisy.

While this was taking place, the Enlightenment Being thought, "As the Pacceka-Buddha said I should, just as he had encouraged me to do, I made an effort to come to this place. Therefore, it is my duty to do meritorious deeds." Thinking so, from that point on he started to do good deeds by giving alms to the needy, and thereby acquired merit from being a righteous king. Finally, he passed on as the king of Gandhāra.

He was I, who am the Buddha today.

The moral: "Yielding to temptations brings harm. Self-control brings rewards."

133

The Story of [Sacrificial Fire] Eating (or, Being Sprinkled with) Ghee
(*Ghatāsana-Jātaka*)

At one time, the omniscient one was living in Jetavana monastery in Sāvatthi. This story was delivered in front of a certain monk who had gone to a remote village to observe the spring retreat.

A certain monk went to observe the spring retreat, and the temple in which he was living burnt down in a fire. When the monk asked his supporters to repair it, those villagers said, "Next week we have to plough." "Next week we have to make a fence." Similarly, giving such various excuses, they could not repair the building for the whole three months. As there were no facilities, the monk could not develop his mind so as to obtain an aura. He wasted his days. And then at the end of the spring retreat, he went to see the Buddha. He knelt down in the presence of the Buddha, and sat by his side.

The omniscient lord had a chat with him about his life during the spring retreat at the remote village. He asked, "Oh monk, how is your progress in meditation? Were you able to do your meditation successfully?" Then the monk said that he was unable to meditate, as there were no facilities in which to do so. Then the Buddha asked, "Why did you not go to a place where facilities were available? It is necessary for you to meditate to overcome defilement. Even birds in the past went away from where they did not have proper facilities to live." Then the Buddha was invited to disclose the past story. Buddha disclosed the past story thus:

There was a king called Brahmadatta who was ruling in the city of Benares long ago. At that time, the Enlightenment Being was a bird, and he became the leader of many birds. They lived on a tree beside a certain river.

Many birds roosted overnight on a branch of the tree that overhung the river, and they dropped their dung into the river. A certain divine cobra that was living in the river got angry because of the fouling of his water. He thought that he would burn the tree so that the birds would not live there any more. One day, when all the birds were roosting on the same branch, the divine cobra puffed out a poisonous steam that boiled the water of the river. Then, he puffed out fire. Because of this, a lot of fire and steam rose high up from the water.

On seeing this strange thing, the Enlightenment Being said to his flock of birds, "It is not good to stay here because from the water, fire has arisen. Therefore, let us go away to another place." Some of the birds did not pay attention to that. Only a few went with him.

The fully enlightened one concluded this story saying, "I, who am now the lord Buddha, was the leader of the birds at that time."

The moral: "One should leave a place that is inhospitable."

134

The Story of Clarifying Mental Absorption [The Story of the Jewel in the Flower]

(*Jhānasodhana-Jātaka, Puppharatna-Jātaka*)

At one time, when Buddha was living in Jetavana monastery, he disclosed this Jātaka. At that time, after the spring retreat of the monks, Buddha descended from heaven to the gate of the town of Saṃkassa. On that day, Venerable Sāriputta very intelligently solved the questions of the monks, which the monks appreciated. With regard to one of the Venerable Sāriputta's solutions of a question, this story was told. This is the story:

Long ago when King Brahmadatta was ruling the city of Benares, the Enlightenment Being was living in the Himalayan forest as a leader of many ascetics.

At that time, the Enlightenment Being's first disciple went to a nearby village to observe the spring retreat. In the meantime, the ascetic Enlightenment Being came to the end of his life. His other disciples came to the dying Enlightenment Being and asked, "Revered one, did you gain any kind of religious success from your practices of mental absorption?"

The Enlightenment Being said, "Nothing, it is not anything [*akiñcanaṃ, natthi kiñci*]." While he was saying this, his consciousness disappeared and he was born in the Brahma world.

The ascetic disciples, on hearing his words, could not understand their meaning. They thought, "Alas. He has been born in a Brahma world where people who have incorrect ideas [*micchā-diṭṭhi*] are born." Thinking so, they did not perform for him an elaborate funeral.

After this, the first chief disciple returned and asked the other ascetics, "What did our master say before his death?"

The other ascetics said what they had heard. Then the chief disciple said, "Oh, if it is so, then there is no doubt he has been born among the resplendent Brahma-s [*ābhassara*-s]." When he said this, the others did not believe him. Then the master who had been born in the Brahma world came down and appeared before them. He said, "My chief disciple has spoken the truth." He then returned to the Brahma world.

The chief disciple ascetic at that time was the Venerable Sāriputta. And I was the master ascetic who was born among the resplendent Brahma-s and who have obtained full enlightenment at the present time.

The moral: "Understanding is appreciated by everyone."

135

The Story of Moonbeams
(*Candābha-Jātaka*)

When the Buddha was living in the Jeta Grove monastery, he delivered this Jātaka story with regard to the Venerable Sāriputta's solving of questions at a time when the Buddha was descending from heaven near the gate of the town of Saṃkassa. This is the story:

At one time, a king called Brahmadatta ruled the city of Benares. At that time, the Enlightenment Being was the master of many ascetics in the Himalayan forest. On the day he was dying, the ascetics came to him and asked, "Revered one, what type of a mental achievement was gained by you?" He said, "The moon's radiance, the sun's radiance." Saying so, he passed away.

Then the chief ascetic disciple, hearing the words of the master ascetic, said, "Our master has been born in the resplendent Brahma world [*ābhassara*]." The other disciples did not accept this. As they were not accepting it, the master who had been born in the Brahma world descended; and he verified that what the chief ascetic disciple had said was indeed so. He then returned to the Brahma world.

The chief disciple at that time was the Venerable Sāriputta. And I was the master ascetic who today has become the supreme being of this world.

The moral: "Truth will be certified by divine beings."

136

The Story of the Golden Swan
(*Suvaṇṇahaṃsa-Jātaka*)

While Buddha was living in Jeta grove at Sāvatthi a certain man devoted to Buddhism cultivated a garden in which he grew garlic, and he gave garlic to many monks. When people requested garlic, he used to give it to them. When the number of people became too many, he used to tell them to go into his garden and take a certain number of handfuls as he had specified. Everything was going well like this for a period of time. Even nuns used to come for garlic, and would take handfuls of cloves as he specified.[15] At one time, a certain nun named Nandā came to his house with other nuns and requested garlic [for medicine?]. He said, "You may take three handfuls of garlic." Misunderstanding him, she and each of the other nuns *each* took three handfuls. The watchman, seeing this, called out, "Why are you making such a mistake, and taking so much of our garlic?" Hearing of this, other nuns rebuked her.

This news went even to the Buddha. The Buddha said, "It is not good for monks and nuns to take anything which is not given." He said further, "Through greed, much will not be gained. Be satisfied with whatever you are given, even if it is a handful." In this way, he emphasized being satisfied with whatever one gets. "Such a one who is satisfied like that, he will gain more than one who is greedy. And what is gained will be permanently with him." In this way, he criticized what the nuns did. Then the Buddha added, "This nun was greedy not only today. Also in the past

15 Garlic is not supposed to be eaten by nuns. In South Asian tradition generally, garlic and onions are considered to make one lusty, and are therefore to be avoided by women, especially widows. Also when one perspires after eating garlic, one gives off a smell that is displeasing to others. Indian law texts also note that garlic and onions are to be avoided by twice-born men.

she was greedy like this." The monks said, "Revered sir, please disclose to us this story." And the Buddha told the story of the past:

At one time in the city of Benares, a king called Brahmadatta was ruling. At the same time, the Enlightenment Being was born in a Brahmin family and had three daughters. One was named Nandā. Another was named Nandavatī. And the third was named Sundarinandā. Unfortunately, before his daughters could be married, the father who was the Enlightenment Being died suddenly. He was born again as a golden swan that had a reminiscence of its preceding life. He understood that prior to this life, he had been born in a Brahmin family. And he learned that his wife and three daughters were living by slavery, and he decided to help them. He thought, "My feathers are golden. Therefore, they are good for making jewelry. So if I go to my wife and children I can give them one feather, for the purpose of making jewelry, every other month." And he went to their home, and sat on the roof. The daughters came out of the house and asked, "Who are you?" He said, "I am your father. I came here to help you and your mother." Saying so, he dropped a golden feather and went away. He did this several times, and each time the daughters picked up the feather. Meanwhile, the Brahmin mother thought, "This bird may change his mind at some point. If he should think in the future that he does not want to come here, then it will be a big hardship for us." Thinking so, she summoned her daughters and said, "One day, catch your father and pluck all his feathers."

On hearing their mother's words, the three daughters said, "If we do so, there is no doubt that our father will feel hurt all over his body. Therefore, we do not want to do so." When they were arguing like this one day, their father came to their home. Then the Brahmin mother said, "Please, husband, come here." In this way, she summoned him near to her. The Enlightenment Being quickly went near to her. The woman immediately seized him and plucked all his feathers from his body.

As his golden feathers were plucked with a bad motive, they became a normal swan's feathers. And he could not fly away as he had no feathers.

He just lay in their home. As time went by his feathers grew again, but as normal white swan's feathers. When this happened, the family let him just fly away.

Afterwards, the Enlightenment Being never came back again to that house.

"Oh, monks. Because of her greed, she lost the chance to get golden feathers." Concluding this story, the Buddha said, "The present nun called Nandā was the former Brahmin woman. The three daughters were this nun's three daughters [who in this life picked garlic with her]. The golden swan was I who have become the enlightened one." In this way, the Buddha concluded the story.

The moral: "Do not pluck fruit from your tree greedily."

137

The Story of the Cats
(*Babbu-Jātaka*)

At one time the enlightened one was living in the Jeta Grove. At that time, there was an enlightened lady called Kāṇā-mātā [Kāṇā's mother]. Why was she known as Kāṇā's mother? Because she had a daughter known as Kāṇā who was so known not because she was blind, but because she was so beautiful. Anyone who saw her was not able to look at another woman [as if they were blind].[16]

Her mother had given her in marriage to someone of a similarly matched family. She lived in that family for a long time without seeing her mother. After a long time, she came to see her mother and spent a long while with her. As she was delaying returning home, her husband sent a message that he wanted her to return home quickly so he could see her. When she heard this message, Kāṇā said to her mother that she had to return home.

Hearing that, her mother, Kāṇā-mātā, said to her that she should not return empty-handed, but should take with her some sweetcakes. When they were preparing these sweetcakes, a monk who was going on his alms round came. The devout Kāṇā-mātā could not say there was nothing to give as she had just prepared sweetcakes. So they gave him a bowl full of sweetcakes. When he was returning to the temple, on his way, he met another monk going on his alms round and said, "Go to Kāṇā-mātā's home. She has sweetcakes."

Hearing that, he also went there and got a bowl full of sweetcakes. In the same way, as he was returning he met still another monk who was

16 Kāṇā means 'blind', usually of one eye, occasionally of both.

going on alms round. He told the same thing to him and to a fourth monk. Now, when they had given sweetcakes to four monks, the sweetcakes were all gone.

As Kāṇā now had nothing to bring for her husband, she postponed her trip. A second time her husband requested her to come home. Also the second time, the sweetcakes were given to the same monks in this way. And again, she could not return home.

As she was not coming home, her husband married another woman. This was heard by Kāṇā, and she started to cry. Kāṇā-mātā was also very upset. The Buddha heard this, and he visited their home, sat on the prepared chair, and asked Kāṇā-mātā, "Devoted lady, why is your daughter crying?" She told the Buddha what had happened. On hearing this, Buddha preached to them in an appropriate way so as to console their grief and then returned to Jetavana monastery.

On the same day, in the evening, the monks assembled in the preaching hall were discussing what had happened because of those four monks and Kāṇā's failure to return home, and how Kāṇā-mātā was upset. Meanwhile, Buddha came there in the evening to preach. He asked the monks, "Oh monks, what were you discussing before I came?" When Buddha heard from them what they had been discussing, he said, "Monks, not only today, but even before these four monks have brought sorrow to Kāṇā-mātā by taking her provisions." The monks requested the Buddha to disclose this. And he explained this story:

Long ago in ancient times there was a king called Brahmadatta in Benares. While he was ruling in Benares, the Enlightenment Being was born in a family of stone-sculptors, and he became a teacher of stone-sculptors. At that time, a millionaire in a remote village who had 40 million crores of gold hidden in a certain place passed away. Later, his wife also passed away while still having a craving for the wealth. She was reborn as a female mouse living in a nearby anthill.

At one point, the Enlightenment Being came to that village, which by that time had been abandoned. Breaking rocks that were there, he took them from that abandoned village and used them for his work. And he supported himself in this way. The female mouse saw the Enlightenment Being coming once a day, and she became enamored of him. She thought, "I have much wealth. By giving my wealth to this man, I also can live a happy life. I will bring him a gold coin each day, and he will bring me good things to eat." Thinking so, one day she brought a gold coin in her mouth, and put it down in front of the Enlightenment Being. Seeing that, he asked, "What is this?" The female mouse said, "Take this money, and bring me some meat. The remainder can be used by your lordship."

In this way, she gave him a gold coin daily. And the Enlightenment Being brought meat, the worth of gold equal in weight to four grains of rice, and gave the meat to the mouse. The balance of the gold he used for his own purposes. As time went on, a cat that was searching for prey saw the mouse, and caught her. The mouse said, "Please let me go." The cat said, "I am searching for something to eat. I caught you so as to eat your flesh." The mouse said, "If you eat me today, then you will have meat for only one day. Is it better to have meat for only one day, or forever?" The cat said, "If I have meat forever, that would be good." When the cat said this, then the mouse said, "If that is so, then please let me go. I will provide you daily with meat." The cat agreed, saying, "Give me meat daily. If you fail to do so, then I know what to do." In this way, he threatened the mouse, and let her go.

Since then, the mouse divided her share of meat that the Enlightenment Being gave her each day into two parts. One part she gave to the cat, and she ate the other part. Unfortunately, on another day, another cat caught her. She promised the same thing as to the first cat, and in this way got let go. In this way, she also saved herself from a third cat and a fourth cat. Having made such promises, she used to divide the meat she obtained into five parts. She ate herself only one part. And she gave the other four parts to the four cats. As she did not have enough food day by day, she became very thin and weak.

The Enlightenment Being, seeing her like this, asked, "Why are you so thin and weak?" She told him what had happened. The Enlightenment

Being said, "Why did you not tell me this up to now?" Saying this, he made a cavity in a block of clear crystal stone. He said, "When the cats come to ask you for meat, insult them while you are inside this crystal cavity." Making her promise to do so, he went away. The mouse went into the hollow of the clear crystal. The first cat came along. He asked, "Where is the meat that you promised to give me?" Then the mouse said, "What? Am I someone who is supposed to give you meat? If you need meat, eat your kittens' flesh." In this way, she insulted him so as to make him angry. The cat got angry and said, "Ah, are you going back on your word in this way?" He then jumped up at the mouse, and not knowing that she was inside a piece of clear crystal, he hit it hard and thereby broke his ribs. He crept away, and died lying in the forest.

In this way, the other three cats as well got angry at the female mouse's words, and jumping up forcefully at the crystal, also ended their lives.

Since then, the female mouse became more and more enamored with the Enlightenment Being. She started to give him two gold coins daily. Doing so, she eventually gave up all her 40 million crores of gold coins.

The Buddha concluded the story, comparing the four cats eating the mouse's meat with the four monks eating the sweetcakes of the devoted Kāṇā-mātā. And the Buddha imposed a regulation on monks not to accept the giving of food by going to a home without invitation, even though a monk might know that there is good food there. If invited, only then can he accept the food.

"At that time, the four cats were these four monks. The female mouse was the devoted lady called Kāṇā-mātā. The stone-sculptor was myself who became in this life the enlightened one." In this way, the Buddha concluded the Jātaka story of the cats.

The moral: "It is not good to take advantage of generous people."

138

The Story of an Iguana
(*Godha-Jātaka*)

The Buddha told this story at Jetavana monastery about a hypocritical monk who understood how to be cunning, as in the past story of the *Kuhaka-Jātaka* [No. 89].

At one time, King Brahmadatta was ruling in Benares. While he was ruling, the Enlightenment Being was born as an iguana. He lived in a termite hill in a remote village.

At the same time, there lived in the same village, with the help of the villagers, a very virtuous and highly righteous ascetic. The Enlightenment Being, who had been born as an iguana, used to listen to his sweet-voiced sermons two times a day. Later, the ascetic left this place and went to the Himalayas after telling his intentions to the villagers. After that, a bogus ascetic came to that village and settled in the same temple. Living there, he accepted the offerings of the villagers.

The iguana, who was the Enlightenment Being, thought that this ascetic would also be righteous like the former ascetic. And he came to see him also two times a day. One day, there was an untimely rain and termites came out in swarms from the locality's termite hills. Many iguanas came out from the various termite hills to eat the termites. The villagers, seeing that there were many iguanas, started to kill them. They then cooked the delicious iguana meat. Some of them gave this as an offering to the bogus ascetic. The ascetic tasted the meat and asked, "What kind of meat is this?" They responded, "It is iguana meat." And the ascetic became intent on eating more iguana meat. He thought, "There is a big iguana that comes to me twice a day. I can kill him, and eat his meat."

Thinking so, he requested the villagers to bring some condiments and a pot with which to cook. He hid them in the temple. Then he made a club that he could use to kill the iguana. He hid the club under his robes, and he sat at the end of the cloister path waiting for the iguana to come while taking a very righteous and virtuous pose.

When the iguana was coming from his termite hill, he sensed a difference in the ascetic. He did not go near to him as before. He first went upwind, and he smelt the smell of iguana meat coming from the robes of the ascetic. Therefore, he did not approach as he had become afraid. Instead, he went around the ascetic. As the iguana did not come near to him, the ascetic became upset. As he was anxious to kill the iguana, he thought that he would now throw the club and hit him from afar. Fortunately, the club missed the iguana, hitting only its tail. For a second time, the bogus ascetic ran to get the club and hit the iguana. The iguana, though, ran into a nearby termite hill and saved his life.

The iguana poked his head out through another hole in the termite hill and said, "Hey, ascetic. I thought that you were a righteous person, like the former ascetic. Such a person as you does not deserve to wear saffron robes and a turban, and to sit on a tiger skin." Saying so, he went to hide.

The ascetic thought, "It is no longer good for me to stay here because the iguana can tell the villagers about me." Thinking so, he left for the Himalayan forest on the very same day.

The Buddha, disclosing this story, said, "This bogus ascetic was the present hypocritical monk. The righteous ascetic was the Venerable Sāriputta. And I was the iguana, who has now become the fully enlightened one."

The moral: "Righteousness can only be known through a long association with someone."

139

The Story of One Who Had Lost in Two Ways
(*Ubhatobhaṭṭha-Jātaka*)

At one time the fully enlightened one was living in the Bamboo Grove. The monks who had assembled in the preaching hall in the evening at one point brought up a discussion about Devadatta. As he was not fulfilling the duties of a monk expounded by the Buddha, he was not truly a monk. He was wandering here and there in the guise of a monk. Also he was not a layman, and he had lost all the gainfulness of a layman. Therefore, he was like firewood that had been burned from both ends and had been smeared with bodily impurities in the middle. He had lost out from both sides, no longer gaining the achievements of a monk nor the perquisites of a member of a royal household.

At this time, the Buddha entered the preaching hall and asked, "Oh monks, what were you discussing before I came?" The monks told the Buddha about their discussion. The Buddha said, "Oh monks, not only today, but even in the past the Venerable Devadatta had lost in two ways." The monks requested the Buddha to disclose the story.

"At one time, King Brahmadatta was ruling the city of Benares. At that time, the Enlightenment Being was born as a tree sprite in a forest near a pond by a remote village.

"A certain fisherman came with his son to fish in the village pond. He put his line and hook in the water in an area where there were many fish. The hook went down and got caught on a root. The fisherman tried his best to pull it out, but could not. He thought, 'No doubt, the bait has been swallowed by a big fish.' He spoke to his son to send a message to his wife to quarrel with the neighbors. Afterward, he tried to pull up the fishing hook. He then thought, 'If I try more, I will break the line.' He took off his clothes and placed them on the bank of the pond. With the intention of catching the fish, he jumped into the water. In the water there were some thistle-like roots that pricked out his eyes, and he became blind. And a robber who was passing by stole his clothes that were on the bank of the pond.

"On hearing her son's words, the mother thought of a way of making a quarrel with the neighbors. She devised a stratagem. She put a palm leaf plug in the pierced hole of one of her ears, applied char from a pot to one of her eyes, and held in her arm a little puppy as if it were a child, pretending that she was mad. The village women said, 'You have gone mad.' She said, 'Not me. You have gone mad.' In this way, she created a quarrel. This quarrel was reported to the village headman. He, on listening to them, blamed her. He fined her, and had her beaten.

"The fisherman came out from the water and searched for his clothes, covering his bleeding eyes with his hand. But he could not find them.

"The Enlightenment Being, who was a tree sprite, was nearby. He said on seeing this, 'Hey, foolish fisherman! Being a foolish man and jumping into shallow water, you wounded your eyes. And you lost your clothes that had been placed on the bank. Your wife, who was at home, was beaten and lost wealth in a fine. Because of your foolishness, you lost out in two ways.' Saying so, the tree sprite disappeared.

"The fisherman who lost his eyes at that time was Devadatta. And the tree sprite was I who am the Buddha." Saying so, the Buddha disclosed the story of one who had lost in two ways.

The moral: "A greedy person gains nothing."

140

The Story of Crows
(*Kāka-Jātaka*)

The enlightened one told this story while he was at Jetavanārāma monastery on a certain occasion when he was assisting his own relatives. Its present story appears in the *Bhaddasāla-Jātaka* in the tenth book [No. 465].

[While Buddha was living in Jetavanārāma, King Kosala wanted to give alms to the monks. But on that day there was not even a single monk in the monastery. The king thought, "I always give alms. But the monks do not have full confidence in me because I am not a relative of the Buddha. If I became a relative, the monks will be more confident in and friendly to me." Therefore, he sent a message to the Sākya king requesting him to give a Sākya virgin princess as his queen. So the Sākya king, who was afraid of the king of Kosala because he was mighty and powerful, thought, "It is good to give a girl to him. But we ought not give him a real Sākya girl. We will give him a half Sākya girl." Thinking so, he gave him the princess Vāsabhakhattiyā, who was the daughter of the Sākya Mahānāma by a slave girl. After she had given birth to a son for him, named Viḍūḍabha, King Kosala eventually came to understand what had happened. At that time, he cut off Vāsabhakhattiyā's and Viḍūḍabha's royal allowances, and treated them as he would slaves. Buddha interceded, and convinced him to reinstate Vāsabhakhattiyā and Viḍūḍabha to their noble status.

Eventually Viḍūḍabha, after he had become king of Kosala, as he harbored resentment toward the Sākyas for their insult to his father, attacked the Sākyas at Kapilavatthu. On the way, three times, Buddha met him and persuaded him not to attack. On the fourth time, the Buddha understood that because of the Sākyas' previous Kamma, he could not prevent the attack. At that time, Viḍūḍabha destroyed all the Sākya families.

This news spread even among the monks. They were discussing this news one day in the Dhamma Hall, saying that the Buddha had not been able to prevent the killing of the Sākyas because of their Kamma, even though he had tried to intercede three times. Three times, however, the Buddha turned back Viḍūḍabha. Fully three times the Buddha tried to save his relatives from danger. Buddha is a helpful friend to his kin.]

Buddha entered and asked, "Oh monks, what were you talking about before I entered?" They said, "Bhante, we were talking about the helpfulness of yourself to your relatives, and the destruction of your relatives." Then the Buddha said, "Monks, not only this time, but even in my previous lives I have been helpful to my relatives, protecting them from danger." The monks said, "Please, Bhante, tell us the past story, as we understand the present." The enlightened one said:

At one time, King Brahmadatta was ruling in Benares. On a certain occasion, his Brahmin advisor was wandering in the street. At that time, there were two crows seated on an archway. One crow said to the other, "I would like to make droppings on this Brahmin." The other crow said, "This Brahmin is a very powerful person. By doing so, you will make him angry. And then he will be angry with us. If he gets angry, there is no doubt that he can kill us all. Therefore, do not do it." The first crow said, "Right now I cannot stop from putting a dropping on him. Therefore, I will do it. Whatever may happen, so be it." The second crow said, "Do whatever you like. The results will come upon you. I am not responsible." Saying this, he went away.

When the Brahmin came to the archway, the crow put droppings on him. The Brahmin, seeing this, got very angry and kept this in his mind.

At that time, a certain slave woman placed a little bit of paddy grain on the ground in the sunshine. A shaggy goat came there, and started to eat the grain. The woman, carrying a club, hit him and chased him away. Several times, the goat came back. Each time, she hit him and chased him away. The last time, the old woman thought, "If this goat comes again to eat my grain, I may lose my profits." So, taking a wooden branding iron in her hand and lying in hiding in a nearby spot, when the goat came again she hit him on his matted hair which caught fire.

The burning goat, thinking of putting out the fire, ran to the king's elephant stables where he saw a pile of hay. He rolled in the hay in order to try to put out the fire. Then the hay started to burn. And the whole elephant stable caught fire and began to burn. The elephants that were tethered there also got burnt and wounded. The king's elephant physicians said that it would be difficult to treat the burnt and wounded elephants. The king summoned his Brahmin advisor, and asked him how to best treat the elephants.

Hearing this, the Brahmin advisor said, "Your lordship, if you can get some crow fat, then I know how to treat them." The king, hearing these words, ordered his subjects to kill crows. In accord with this order, all citizens who lived in the city started to kill thousands of crows and made a pile of crow carcasses.

At this time, the Enlightenment Being was a king of a large group of 84,000 crows that lived near a certain cemetery. This king of crows heard the news. He thought, "It is my responsibility to save the lives of my relatives. No one else can do it." So he, thinking of his fulfillment of the ten-fold perfections and the spreading of his loving kindness upon all living beings, said to his subjects, "I have heard that our relatives are being killed by the king. I am going to protect my relatives. Everyone will have to come with me. If this determination of mine to save their lives is in accord with truth [*sacca*], no harm will come to anyone." With such a determination, he quickly went to the king's palace. Through an open window he entered the king's palace and perched atop the king's throne.

Then one of the king's security men saw the crow and came near to seize him. At this point, the crow said to the king, "Your lordship, is it good to do something just on the basis of a man's word without looking into the truth of it? It is a very bad thing to kill all crows. It is not good for a king to act from anger. A king must examine things before he does them." Hearing these words pleased the king. He entertained the Enlightenment Being by applying to his feathers medicinal oil prepared with hundreds of medicines, which made the Enlightenment Being very strong, and by feeding the Enlightenment Being food prepared for himself. The king laid out for the Enlightenment Being a golden cloth on which to sit, and asked him, "Why is it that crows have no fat? [I have had thousands of crows killed, and yet have obtained no crow fat.]"

The Enlightenment Being started to talk, his voice resonating through the whole palace building. "Your lordship, when a crow sees a human being, even a little child, he is afraid of him and flies away since he is always threatened by humans. Because of this, there is no fat in the body of a crow since he is living with fear, be it in the present, the past, or the future. Your Brahmin advisor wanted to destroy the entire community of crows as he was angry with us." And he explained the story to the king. The king became very sad, and was pacified toward all crows. The king was very pleased with the Enlightenment Being, and said, "I would like to offer you my kingdom as a gift. Please accept it." The Enlightenment Being said, "Your lordship, what is the advantage to me in having a kingdom? Be kind enough just to let my relatives live freely in *your* kingdom."

The king, who was pleased with the words of the crow, gave freedom in his kingdom to *all* living beings. He especially advised his subjects not to kill any crows. And further, every day he laid out for the crows six bushels of variously delicately flavored cooked rice. In this way, the king did very many meritorious deeds. He eventually died according to the results of his previous deeds.

"The king of Benares at that time was the Venerable Ānanda. And I who am now the Buddha was the king of crows." Saying so, the Buddha disclosed the Jātaka story of crows.

The moral: "Anger and vengeance cause fear and unhappiness. Loving kindness and compassion bring fearlessness and peace."

141

The Story of an Iguana
(*Godha-Jātaka*)

When the Buddha was living in the Bamboo Grove, he disclosed this Jātaka story because of a certain disobedient monk. The present story for the reason behind this story was explained in detail in the *Mahilāmukha-Jātaka* [No. 26].

At one time, King Brahmadatta was ruling in Benares. At that time, the Enlightenment Being was born as an iguana with a following of thousands of iguanas. They lived in a big termite hill.

The Enlightenment Being had a son who was friendly with a chameleon. On seeing this, many iguanas complained about it to the Bodhisatta. The Bodhisatta summoned his son, and warned him not to be friendly with the chameleon. Because of such a friendship, there would be a great disaster for the community of iguanas. Even though he was so warned, the young iguana did not listen to him. He continued to play with the chameleon, and they continued to embrace each other. In the course of time, the iguana became large and fat. Bearing such a heavy body, when the iguana embraced the chameleon the big-bodied iguana sometimes hurt the chameleon, who had a small body. The small chameleon perceived the play of the iguana to be as if a big rock were falling over his body. And he became angry.

The king of the iguanas, in doubt about his son's continued relationship with the chameleon, thought that one day calamity might befall upon the community of iguanas. He therefore made a secret tunnel so as to be able to flee away.

In the meantime, there came a certain unexpected rain. Swarms of flying termites came out from the termite hill. On a certain iguana hunter's seeing this, he thought, "Now is a good time to hunt, because iguanas come out to eat flying termites." So thinking, he entered the forest. While he was wandering in the forest, the chameleon saw him and enquired as to why he was wandering in the forest. The hunter said, "I am searching for iguanas." As the chameleon was angry with his friend, the iguana, he said, "Do not be bothered by searching for iguanas. I can show you a place where there are plenty. What you need is some hay and fire." Hearing this, the hunter brought some hay and fire. When he did this, the chameleon said, showing him the termite hill hole, "Put hay inside it and set it on fire. When the smoke goes in, the iguanas will come out. When they come out, hit them with your club or chase after them with your dogs. You can easily kill as many as you want." The hunter did this.

The Enlightenment Being thought, "This type of a calamity came upon my relatives because of the evil chameleon."

The Enlightenment Being fled away through the secret tunnel.

"The chameleon at that time was Devadatta. The disobedient little iguana was this monk today who is disobedient. And I who have now obtained supreme Buddhahood was at that time the king of the iguanas." Saying so, the Buddha ended this Jātaka story of an iguana.

The moral: "Choose your friends wisely."

142

The Story of a Jackal
(*Sigāla-Jātaka*)

When the Enlightenment Being was living in the Bamboo Grove temple of Rājagaha, one day old monks assembled in the preaching hall and were discussing Devadatta's attempts to kill the Buddha. They said, "Devadatta sent the elephant Nāḷāgiri to kill the Buddha, but he failed to do so. Then he tried to kill him by pushing rocks from Gijjhakūṭa Mountain. And then he sent bowmen to shoot at him. With many such strategies, he was not able to kill the Buddha." While they were discussing this, the Buddha entered the hall and asked, "Monks, what were you talking about before my arrival?" The monks answered, "Revered one, we were discussing about the attempts of Devadatta to assassinate the Buddha." The Buddha said, "Oh monks, it is not only in this life that Devadatta has tried to kill me. Even in the past he tried and could not do so." The monks invited the Buddha to disclose the ancient story. The Buddha then delivered this story of the past:

At one time, King Brahmadatta was ruling in Benares. At that time, the Enlightenment Being was born a jackal. He lived in a certain cemetery followed by thousands of jackals. Once there was a certain festival in Benares for which people prepared plenty of meat and toddy that they kept everywhere here and there. The people partied day and night until midnight. But they could not finish the prepared toddy. One man came asking for meat and toddy. Many people said, "There is no more meat." But a certain man said, "While I am here, why do you say there is no meat?" Saying so, he took a club. As the gates of the city were closed, he went out through the sewer ditches, and went to a nearby cemetery. He lay down on the cemetery ground as if he were a dead body. In the meantime, the Enlightenment Being, who was a jackal, went to eat meat. He saw this man lying there and thought, "No doubt, this man is not dead. Nevertheless, it would be wise to test it." Thinking so, he went to the opposite side of the wind and smelling, he found out that the man was not dead. Thinking that he would make the man look foolish, so as to deceive the man he made as if he were running away. Then he went near to the club. He took it in his mouth and pulled on it. The man who was holding it, pulled back on it. Then the jackal went away a little bit, and said, "It is difficult to know whether someone who is lying down is dead or alive. But when the club is pulled back, how can that person be dead? He is not even sleeping."

The man got up and got angry. He threw the club toward the jackal, but missed. He said, "You got away from me!" Then the jackal said, "Yes. I survived! But you will not survive from the four-fold hell!"

Then that man went back alone to the city in the same way as he had come. He entered the city and washed off both himself and his soiled and dirty clothing in the city moat.

At that time the man who went to kill the Enlightenment Being, who was then a jackal, was Devadatta. And I who was born as the king of jackals am today the Buddha.

The moral: "Ill-conceived stratagems cannot deceive a wise person, no matter what his station."

143

The Story of Shining Forth
(*Virocana-Jātaka*)

At one time when Buddha was living at the Jeta Grove, Devadatta came to the Buddha and requested him to impose four new practices on all the monks. The first was that all monks should wear robes stitched together from the clothing of the departed that could be picked up in the cemetery. The second was that all monks should live under trees, not in houses. The third was that monks should not eat meat or fish during their lifetime. The fourth was that monks should live all the time in the forest, not in a village or city. The Buddha responded that he had monks in his community who had been very rich, and who had before their ordination comfortable lives. Therefore, those who wish to do as Devadatta suggests, let them do it. Those who do not so wish, let them not do it. He was not going to impose such regulations as might be objectionable to them. Devadatta got angry because the Buddha refused to do as he wanted. He took away 500 monks who were followers of the Venerable Sāriputta and who had only recently been ordained, and went with them to Gayāsīsa. He said that he had not gotten anything from the Buddha, not even a blade of grass. And he created a schism in the order. With the 500 monks, he went to Gayāsīsa north of the Ganges River, and claimed there that he also was a Buddha.

At one point, the Buddha came to understand that the 500 monks who had gone off with Devadatta had the potentiality at that time of becoming Arahants on account of their previous births. Understanding so, the Buddha summoned the Venerable Sāriputta and Moggallāna and requested that they go to Devadatta's community and preach to the 500 monks, bringing them back into the Buddha's fold. Then the two chief disciples of the Buddha, Sāriputta and Moggallāna, left for Devadatta's community.

Devadatta saw from afar the two chief disciples coming toward him, and he imagined that they were giving up the Buddha, and were coming to join his community. Thinking so, he claimed that like the Buddha he too had back pain. He requested that in his stead, they might preach to the community. He lay down near the preaching chair and went to sleep. The Venerable Sāriputta preached then, and all the 500 monks attained Arahant-ship. They all then returned with him and Moggallāna to the Buddha at the Bamboo Grove.

Kokālika, the chief disciple of Devadatta, came to Devadatta's temple and saw that it was empty of people. He went into the temple, and saw Devadatta sleeping there. He got angry and said to Devadatta, "You are sleeping deeply while your disciples have been taken away by the two chief disciples of the Buddha. Our temple is empty now." With his left foot, he kicked Devadatta's chest. This caused Devadatta to vomit blood.

When the Venerable Sāriputta and Moggallāna came to the Buddha with the 500 monks, the Buddha asked, "How was Devadatta when you were there?" The Venerable Sāriputta said, "Revered one, when we were there, Devadatta was pretending to be a Buddha. He was preaching." And Sāriputta then explained all that had happened, including Devadatta's being kicked by Kokālika. The Buddha heard that news and said, "Sāriputta, not only today, but also in the past has Devadatta imitated me. And by doing so, he fell into a big calamity." The Venerable Sāriputta then invited the Buddha to disclose the former story.

This is how it was:

At one time, King Brahmadatta was ruling in Benares. At that time, the Bodhisatta was born as a lion. He lived in a den hollowed into a big rock.

One day, he left his den and killed a water buffalo, eating the meat. He went to a nearby pool and drank some water. Returning to his den, he met a jackal. The jackal did not see the lion till the lion came very close.

He became very much afraid as he had no way of fleeing. Kneeling down, he paid obeisance to the lion. The lion said, "Jackal! Why do you want to kneel down like that?" The cunning jackal said, "Oh, your lordship. I did so, as I would like to serve you." The lion, who was the Enlightenment Being, then took him to his den in the rock and showed him a place to lie down. He said, "Whenever you see any animal you would like to eat in this area, let me know. Then I will kill him, and we will both have food to eat." The jackal said, "Yes, sir."

The jackal followed this advice. And the jackal and lion both ate the same food. As the jackal got enough food from the lion's killing animals, he became very fat and strong. He then became conceited. "The lion is a beast. I also am a beast. Why should I eat meat killed by someone else? I will kill animals for myself." Thinking so, he went to the lion and said, "Your lordship! I have eaten the meat of the animals that you killed. From now on whatever you kill, you can eat yourself." The lion said, "But you cannot kill animals such as elephants, as I do." He said this several times. Even though the lion prevented the jackal from hunting on its own several times, the jackal did not want to listen. Eventually, the lion said, "Let him learn a lesson." The jackal said, "You should not go to hunt in the morning. I will go." The lion agreed.

In the morning, the jackal got up and came out from the den. He shook his body three times, as the lion always did. And as the lion always roared, he shouted. As the lion would do, he looked in the four directions and he saw an elephant. He ran, and jumped up on the elephant.

When he jumped up on the elephant, he could not remain on the elephant's back. He fell down in front of the elephant. The angry elephant crushed him under his foot. He trampled the carcass, collected the bones in one pile, dropped dung on them, and urinated on them. Then he trumpeted, and went away.

The lion saw this and thought, "The jackal deserved this lesson." Thinking so, he went into his den and sat down.

"The jackal who was crushed by the elephant at that time was Devadatta. And I, who today am the Buddha, the enlightened one, was the lion at that time." Saying so, he ended the Jātaka story of shining forth.

The moral: "One must be true to his nature."

144

The Story of a Tail
(*Naṅguṭṭha-Jātaka*)

At one time Buddha was living in the Jeta Grove. Behind the Jeta grove temple, there was a community of Nigaṇṭha ascetics. They did austerities, claiming that these gained them merit. Among them, some ascetics were standing on one leg only with the other leg raised high, some were squatting on their heels, some were balancing themselves on their toes, and some were lying between four fires and looking up at the sun at midday—which penance they called Pañcatāpa [five scorchings]. They made vows to practice such penances.

Many monks saw these naked ascetics practicing such vows. On seeing this, they came to the Buddha and asked, "Venerable sir, these naked ascetics are practicing such-and-such vows, saying they are doing these in the name of penance. By doing these, do they have any benefit in the future?" The Buddha replied, "Oh monks, what kind of a benefit can be gained by such vows? In the ancient times, even some noble ones taking their birth-fire went into the forest thinking that if they protected that fire, there would be future benefits. They protected that fire for long times, and gained nothing. Giving that up afterwards, they practiced meditation. As a result of that practice, they gained mental absorption and gained a more powerful mental status, and were reborn in the Brahma realm."

How it was:

At one time, a king called Brahmadatta ruled Benares. At that time, the Enlightenment Being was born in a well-known Brahmin family. The Brahmin family preserved the Enlightenment Being's birth-fire for twelve years. When he became twelve years old, his parents said, "Our son, this fire we have protected from your birth to the present. It is more powerful than sacred fire. Take this fire, and go into the forest and offer it to the god of fire. By so offering it, you can gain merit to go to the Brahma world. Whenever you do so, if you would like to go to the Brahma world, stay in the forest and protect that fire. If you want to marry a girl and live a lay life, you can instead do so." On hearing this, the Enlightenment Being thought, "What is the use of a lay life to me? Instead, I will take my birth-fire, go to the forest, and I will sacrifice to the god of fire."

While he was living in the forest, one day he went to a remote village collecting alms. He was given a bull as an offering. He took the bull to the forest with happiness, thinking he would be able to make a good sacrifice to the god of fire. When he returned to his hermitage, he tied the bull to a nearby tree, and he was getting ready to sacrifice the bull to the god. But he found that he did not have salt and lemon juice so as to make the offering tasty. So he went back to the village in search of salt and lemons.

While he was away from his hermitage, unfortunately there came some aboriginal hunters who saw this bull that had on it much meat. They killed the bull on the spot, used the ascetic's birth-fire to cook the meat, and ate as much as they could. Leaving the four legs and the tail, they left carrying away all the remainder of the bull.

The Enlightenment Being, who was the ascetic at that time, returned home carrying salt and lemons so as to sacrifice the bull. He saw his fire, and near it he saw the remaining four legs of the bull and the tail. He saw the bull had been eaten. On seeing this, he got very angry. He realized that there was no use in protecting the fire, as it did not have even the little power to protect the bull that was going to be sacrificed to it. Realizing this, he put out the fire, saying, "Why did I protect this fire as it does not even have the power to protect its own sacrifice? It is not good to help such a powerless god who is not grateful enough to help even its protector. How can it protect me if it cannot protect its own sacrifice?"

He gave up his practice of maintaining his birth-fire. He put it out using the hair on the end of the bull's tail and water. He began to meditate, and through his meditation he was capable of developing concentration in his mind. Later, in the course of time, he was clever enough to obtain the five higher knowledges [*pañcābhiññā*] — miraculous knowledge, divine eye, divine ear, thought reading, and knowledge of reminiscence, and the eightfold mental absorptions [*aṭṭha-samāpatti*]—first mental absorption [*paṭhama-jhāna*], second mental absorption [*dutiya-jhāna*], third and fourth mental absorptions [*tatiya-* and *catuttha-jhāna*], mental absorption of the emptiness, mental absorption of consciousness, mental absorption of nothingness, and mental absorption of neither perception nor non-perception. In the end, he died without falling from the mental absorptions. Maintaining his absorptions, he gained birth in the Brahma world.

"The ascetic of that time was I who am today the Buddha." Saying so, he ended this Jātaka story of a tail.

The moral: "Blind faith can mislead even the wise."

145

The Story of Rādha
(*Rādha-Jātaka*)

At one time when Buddha was living in the Jeta grove, one monk who was infatuated with his former wife after his ordination was ready to disrobe. Buddha heard this. The reason for disclosing the following Jātaka story comes in the *Indriya-Jātaka* [No. 423] further on.

[At one time, a householder when he was advanced in years wanted to give up his lay life and be ordained. When he was ordained, he felt that it was difficult to lead a life without a woman as in monkhood. According to his foolish thought of becoming a layman again, the chief ascetic said, "If you disrobe, you will have to suffer a lot. ..." Finally, the monk who wanted to disrobe realized, as his teacher had explained, "If I go and live a lay life again, I will have to kill animals for meat. Then I will be reborn in hell and I will have to suffer. In my lay life, my present physical strength will not last forever. I will suffer when I am physically weak." Thinking such thoughts, he gave up his thought to be a layman and he began to meditate as before. He knelt down, begging pardon in the presence of his teacher, and he started to meditate. ... Finally, he meditated and learned to control his lust, he gained mental absorption, and he was reborn in the Brahma world.]

To the monk who had become infatuated with his former wife and was trying to disrobe, the Buddha said, "Not only in this life are you trying to do this, but such was so also in a former life. Even in the past, you could not control your unwholesome lust. Therefore it is not surprising that you have such urges." Saying so, the other monks requested the Buddha to disclose the past story, and Buddha related this story:

At one time, a king called Brahmadatta was ruling in Benares. At that time, the Enlightenment Being was born as a parrot.

A Brahmin captured the Enlightenment Being, who was a parrot, and his younger brother also. He brought them to his home. The Enlightenment Being was named Poṭṭhapāda, and his brother was named Rādha. He brought both up as his own children.

Once, the Brahmin wanted to leave his home on business. He summoned his two parrot children and said to them, "If your Brahmin mother does something wrong when I am gone, you must admonish her not to do so. If you do not think you can stop her misconduct, say nothing." Saying so, he left.

From that time, there were limitless people coming in and going out of the house. On seeing this, the Enlightenment Being's brother said to the Enlightenment Being, "When the Brahmin left, he asked us to admonish his wife if there was any wrongdoing. Shall I admonish her?" The Enlightenment Being parrot said, "My brother, you are not yet matured. You say this because you do not understand, and have no experience with women. During the ten hours of the morning, the number of men who come here are not countable. In the ten hours of the afternoon, it is also difficult to say the number of those people who come. Therefore, in such a situation, what advice can we give?" He asked his younger brother, therefore, not to speak. After a few days, the Brahmin returned.

When the Brahmin returned, he asked the Enlightenment Being, "How was my wife's behavior?" The Enlightenment Being said, "There was a myriad of bad behavior. She behaved in this way because she does not love you. Therefore, it is not good to keep her in your home." He further said, "From this point on, it is not good for myself and my brother to stay here." And he thought that he should leave. He summoned his younger brother, went to the Brahmin, knelt down in homage, and begged pardon for his faults. They then returned to the forest.

The Buddha finalized this story, saying, "The Brahmin woman at that time was the former wife of the monk today. The Brahmin was this monk. The parrot Rādha, the younger brother, was the Venerable Ānanda. And the parrot Poṭṭhapāda was I who am today the Buddha."

The moral: "Misplaced lust will not bring you to the correct path."

146

The Story of a Crow
(*Kāka-Jātaka*)

At one time Buddha was living in the Jeta Grove monastery. There was a group of aged gentlemen landowners, and jointly they did meritorious deeds. One day, they got together and while they were chatting, they thought that as they were in old age it would be good to become ascetics, and by doing so they would be able to obtain Arahantship [sainthood]. They approached the Buddha and said, "Venerable sir, kindly ordain us. If you can do so, it would be a great thing for us." Buddha agreed to their request, and they were ordained.

After their ordination, they made little huts for themselves beside Jetavanārāma. And as they had been ordained in old age, they could not study anything. Even by practicing meditation in accord with the Buddha's guidance, they failed to achieve any results.[17] When they went on alms rounds, they usually went to their own former family members' homes. They would take what they obtained to the home of the former wife of the chief monk of the group and eat it there, obtaining from her special sauces cooked by her for their food. In the course of time, this chief monk of the group's wife fell into sickness and died. On hearing this news those old monks, lamenting that the old woman who was skilled in cooking had now passed away, started to cry together.

While they were crying together, other monks heard their cries and came to see what the trouble was. They asked the old monks why they

17 When a person gets old, his mind is not as sharp as when he was young, his memory does not work as well, and he cannot concentrate the same as a young person. Because of this, it is difficult for him to study or meditate. Ideally, a person should be ordained when he is young.

were crying. The old monks said, "We cry because our benefactress who was clever in cooking sauces for us has died. It is because of this that we cry." After hearing this, the monks who came in the evening to the preaching hall were talking about this when the Buddha entered. Buddha asked, "Monks, what were you talking about before my coming?" The monks mentioned the news about the passing away of the wife of the chief monk of the group of old monks, and how the old monks were crying.

Then the Buddha said, "Oh monks, this old chief monk and the group of old monks cry not only in this life. They did so even in the past when the old chief monk's wife died, and they were trying to bail out the water from the ocean and they failed to do it. At that time, because of the help of a good advisor they did not die on account of their futile exertions." The monks requested the Buddha to disclose the past story.

The Buddha said:

At one time, King Brahmadatta was ruling in Benares. At that time, the Enlightenment Being was born as a divine being of the ocean.

Once, some people got together and made offerings to deities and Nāga-s who lived in the ocean with rice, meat, and alcoholic beverages in accord with vows they had made. They placed all these food items on the sand of the beach. When they left, a certain crow and his hen, wandering on the sand, saw these food items there and ate and drank as much as they could. They became intoxicated thereby from both the alcoholic beverages and the rich food. Because they were intoxicated, they decided, using poor judgment, to take a bath in the ocean. While they were bathing in the ocean, a big wave came. It swept the hen-crow out to sea, and a big fish came and swallowed her. On seeing this, the male crow thought that a wave had swallowed his hen. He cried with sorrow.

When they heard his cries, other crows came around and they asked, "Why are you crying?" He told them, "Your friend, the hen-crow who was my wife, was taken by the ocean." The other crows also became very upset. They said, "We have such a large number of crows here. Why should we not just bail the water out of the ocean?"

They then all got together and started to bail out the water of the ocean with their beaks. In this way, they tried for a long time to empty the ocean until they became tired. They then stopped to rest on the sand of the beach, with their beaks being sore from the salty water, their throats being dry, their cheeks being irritated, and their eyes being red from having gotten salt water in them. Very tired from their task, they began to cry, "We have lost our beautiful hen-crow who had a beautiful beak like a parrot, a beautiful color like a peacock, and a sweet voice like a cuckoo. Our beautiful hen-crow was stolen by the thief-like ocean." Saying so, they cried in one voice.

The Enlightenment Being, who had been born as a divine being of the ocean, on hearing the noise of the crows, assumed a dreadful disguise as a bird of prey. Coming there, he made them go away. In this way, he stopped them from being sad any longer.

The Buddha said:

The hen-crow at that time was the dainty woman who today cooked sauces for the old monks. The male crow was the chief monk of the group of old monks. The other crows were the group of old monks. And the divine being of the ocean of whom they were made to be afraid, thereby causing them to fly away, was I who am today the Buddha.

Thus he finished the story.

The moral: "Grieving for the lost is vain."

Also,

"Think before acting out of grief."

147

The Story of Safflower
(*Puppharatta-Jātaka*)

At one time the Buddha was living in Jetavanārāma in Sāvatthi. He disclosed this Jātaka story on seeing a monk disturbed by infatuation with his former wife. The Buddha asked him, "Why, monk, have you become so disturbed with infatuation?" He said, "Your lordship, my former wife is very clever in cooking the daintiest foods, and in other womanly household arts." The Buddha said, "Oh monk, because of her you were impaled in the past, and suffered rebirth in hell." On hearing these words, the other monks requested the Buddha to disclose the story of the past.

This is how the Buddha stated the story:

At one time, King Brahmadatta was ruling the kingdom of Benares. At this time, the Enlightenment Being was born as an aerial deity. Once, when people were celebrating the summer Kattikā festival, a certain poor man in the city had only one cloth to wear for both him and his wife for the festival. Just before the festival, he tore the cloth into two pieces, washed and dried them, and folded them over and over a hundred times until they were small. On the first festival day, he took them out, unfolded them, and gave one of the pieces of cloth to his wife to wear. She said, "I would like to have a cloth to wear that is colored with safflower. While wearing such a safflower-colored cloth, I want to go into the street with you and kiss you." The husband said, "What are you saying? I am a poor man. I do not have safflower-colored cloth. Here is the white cloth that I kept clean after washing it. Wear this cloth as your skirt, and let us go and play in the street." Then his wife said, "No. I do not want to go and play without wearing a safflower-colored cloth. If you want to play in the street with a woman wearing a white cloth, then take your cloth to another woman, and play with her."

On hearing this, he pleaded with her again and again. His wife said, "If a man has a will, what can he not do. Why cannot you go to the king's flower garden and bring some flowers from his garden?" The husband said, "Oh, what are you saying? I not only cannot bring flowers from the king's garden. I cannot even see it." The wife said, "Why cannot you steal some flowers during the night?" Then, on account of his wife's pleading, the husband could not say "no" to her. Finally, he agreed to go and steal the flowers. He went out from the city to the king's flower garden, and jumped up on the fence surrounding it. The security guards heard the noise from this, and went to where he was. They seized the husband, handcuffed him, and the next morning they took him to the king. The king sentenced him to death saying, "Why do you show him to me? Take him, go to the execution ground, and impale him." The guards took him to the execution ground while the execution drums were being beaten, and impaled him alive on a stake. He suffered the pains of the impaling, and while he was still living, crows came and pecked out his eyes. Even though the pain was very severe, he could not stop thinking about his wife. He thought, "All my good wife wanted to do was to go to the festival and enjoy herself while wearing a safflower-colored cloth." While he was thinking such thoughts, he died and was reborn in the hell where there is burning fire.

The husband and wife at that time are today this monk and his former wife. The aerial deity who saw this happen as it was is today the Buddha who preaches to you now.

The moral: "Unending craving causes much suffering."

148

The Story of a Jackal
(*Sigāla-Jātaka*)

The Buddha disclosed this Jātaka story while he was in the Jetavanārāma in Sāvatthi. While he was there in Jetavanārāma, there were 500 new monks who had just come into the order. In the middle of a certain night, in all their minds, they all had lustful thoughts. Buddha, at that same time, was examining the minds of his disciples, thinking out of compassion, "What do my disciples have on their minds?" He realized that these 500 new monks all had lustful thoughts, and he thought, "This is as if a group of enemies have entered into a Universal Monarch's city. While I am living in my temple, these monks have developed lustful thoughts in their minds. I have to remove these lustful thoughts immediately by preaching to them." Thinking so, he addressed the Venerable Ānanda.

Venerable Ānanda was the Buddha's chief attendant for 25 years. Among other things, he helped the Buddha by watching over the temple during the night. He was guarding the temple, walking around carrying a lamp in his hand. On hearing the Buddha address him, he came to the Buddha and said, "Yes, sir." Meanwhile, the Buddha was thinking, "It would be good to summon all those monks who were experiencing confusion, and it would be good to preach to them to eliminate their unwholesome thoughts. But if I preach to them, they will know that the Buddha realized that they had bad thoughts on their minds, and they will be agitated on account of that. They will not be able to listen to the Dhamma. When the mind is agitated, it cannot realize the Dhamma. My preaching will not help them realize a higher state. Therefore, I will preach to all the monks at the same time." He then asked the Venerable Ānanda to summon all the monks.

Hearing the Buddha's words, the Venerable Ānanda took the keys for the doors of all the chambers in the monastery, and went from door to door informing everyone of the Buddha's request. The monks all came to the preaching hall where the Buddha was like a golden rock covered by a golden cloth, and they paid obeisance to him by kneeling down, and then sat around him.

The Buddha was shining with rays of the six colors,[18] which became like an aura around him equal in brightness to a thousand suns and a thousand moons. Sitting, with such an appearance, he started to preach. "Oh, monks, there are three types of thoughts that monks must not think—lustful thoughts, angry thoughts, and injurious thoughts. If you think even a little about women, it may cause you to acquire much demerit. The reason is this: If a snake bites you the wound is very small, but the venom goes through your whole body and kills you. From a small place where lightning has struck, many trees and creepers may be caused to burn and turn into ashes. Lustful thoughts and women are also like that. By being attached to women, the same thing may happen as what happened to a jackal who became attached to an elephant carcass that he thought could give him unlimited meat." The monks asked about the story of the jackal. The Buddha then disclosed this story of the past:

At one time when King Brahmadatta was ruling in Benares, the Enlightenment Being was born as a jackal living in the forest. Once, he saw the dead body of an elephant lying in the forest. He thought, "This is enough food for me to eat for my whole lifetime. I would not have to go anywhere else in search of food. Thinking so, he approached the elephant carcass and took a bite of the trunk. It felt as if he were biting a plough handle. Then he bit the tusk. It felt as if it were the hard core of hard wood. Then he bit the stomach. It felt as if it were bamboo matting. Then he bit the anus. It felt like an oil cake. Then he was satisfied, thinking that he had finally found soft meat. He then ate his way into the belly and decided he could live there as if in a den with plenty of meat to eat and

18 The six colors are blue, yellow, red, white, amber, and all the colors mixed.

blood to drink. When he got sleepy, he would place his head on the lungs as if two pillows and he would lie on the liver as if it were a soft mattress. While he was living like this he thought, "Why should I ever leave this place?" He decided to live inside the elephant carcass permanently, and he spent days on end in it.

After such a situation went on for days on end, there came a severe drought. The elephant's skin dried, and shrunk. The whole carcass of the elephant also dried up and shrunk. The meat became very tough and there was no longer any blood. Inside, the hollow in which he was living became dark as if it were the dark space between worlds. The jackal became afraid, and started to think about a way to get out. He could not find an exit, and so he ran to and fro, and jumped up and down, until he became exhausted. In the meantime, there was a rainfall. The elephant carcass became wet and absorbed water, and light came through the hole through which he had originally entered like a star. The jackal backed up as far as the head of the elephant and darted toward the hole with all his strength as fast as he could. When he jumped like that, all the fur from his body stuck inside the hole in the elephant and his body became smooth like the skin of a Palmyra palm. Seeing his body like this, be became fearful and thought, "Due to my strong craving, I have become like this. I will never again be greedy or eat meat from an elephant carcass."

Saying this, the Buddha preached the four noble truths. He finalized this story, emphasizing them.

After the disclosure of this Jātaka story, the 500 monks, ending their old defilements, became Arahant-s. Other monks attained to the mental status of those who have entered the stream entrance state of mind [*sotāpanna*-s], of those who have attained the once-returner state of mind[19] [*sakadāgāmin*-s], and of those who have attained the non-returner state of mind[20] [*anāgāmin*-s], and this Dhamma sermon further became very helpful to many others.

---

19 That is, of those who will not be reborn on earth more than once.

20 That is, of those who do not return, those who are not reborn.

The Buddha added, "I was born as the jackal at that time."

The moral: "Uncontrolled greed leads to difficulty."

149

The Story of One Leaf [The Story of Shining Forth]

(*Ekapaṇṇa-Jātaka, Virocana-Jātaka*)

When the Buddha was living in the city of Vesāli, he lived in the mansion called, "The Gabled House". At that time, the city of Vesāli was surrounded by three walls each the distance of sixteen Gāvuta-s[21] one from the other, and each having gates and watchtowers. In addition there were 7,707 crowned kings to rule the country, with an equal number of viceroys, generals, and treasurers. Among these there was one bad prince, who was known as Wicked [Duṭṭha]. He was aggressive, rough, and if one would speak something to him he would use insulting words toward that one. Everyday he was like a snake that had been beaten with a stick. He was consumed with anger, and this shone forth to others. When people came to see him, they did not get a chance to speak more than two or three words. Parents, younger brothers, other relatives, and even his own children were uncomfortable in his presence. His wife and all his friends were afraid of him as if he were a snake that bit off flesh little piece by little piece, or as if they had come to a forest in which there were thieves, or as if they had seen a demon. Every time they saw him, they were in fear.

On hearing of this from someone, the Buddha went to see him and advised him: "A man who behaves fiercely like you, no doubt will be reborn in the fourfold hell and suffer from birth to birth. When people get angry, their face is unpleasant looking even though it had been beautiful like a lotus. It looks like a golden mirror covered with filth. In such anger,

21 1 *Gāvuta* = ¼ *yojana*, or a little less than 2 miles.

men hit themselves, or die by hanging themselves with a rope around the neck, or die falling down off a high precipice. By whatever way he dies, in his next birth he will be reborn in hell. After suffering a lot in hell, whenever he gets a human birth he will suffer from the day of his birth with eye diseases, ear diseases, and so forth, endlessly. If he lives with loving kindness toward living beings, or with gentleness, compassion, and kindness, then he will not be confronted with such situations. He will be able to enjoy all kinds of happiness without such sufferings."

From the time the prince heard this, he gave up his pride and anger. He became gentle and restrained like a cobra whose venom had been extracted, like a crab whose claw had been broken, and like a bull with cut horns. If someone hit him, or hurt him, or verbally abused him, he kept silent, not even asking whom it was who did this. If someone behind him mocked him or laughed at him, he did not even turn his head to see who it was. He behaved in this way from that point on.

One day the monks assembled in the preaching hall were talking about this. One monk said, "It is amazing that even his parents constantly advising the prince could not change him. But the Buddha tamed him with a single admonition as a mahout tames an elephant." Then another monk said, "It is commendable, of course, that a horse trainer breaking in his horse guides his horse from east to west, and south to north, according to his will. Just so an elephant trainer and an ox trainer. Also, in the same way, the Buddha goes to wherever there are beings, whether in the human world, heaven, or the Brahma world, and guides them aright. Who can do like that except the Buddha?" Then the Buddha entered, and said, "Oh monks, what were you talking about before I came?" The monks told him they were talking about the taming of the prince. The Buddha said, "Not only today, even in the past I tamed him with a single admonition." And the monks invited the Buddha to disclose the hidden story.

The Buddha disclosed the story:

At one time King Brahmadatta was ruling the city of Benares. At that time the Enlightenment Being was born in a well-known Brahmin family. After his parents' death, he renounced their wealth and went to the Himalayan Mountains to become an ascetic. After a while, he returned to Benares in search of salt and sours.[22] He wandered the streets of Benares for alms.

The king saw him walking on the street and sent one of his ministers to bring him. The minister went to him and told him of the king's invitation. The ascetic said to the minister, "Sir, I have no previous acquaintance with the king. I live in the Himalayan Mountains as an ascetic. Further, since I am an ascetic, I have no close association with him. Therefore, why should he invite me to his palace?"

Hearing this, the minister returned to the palace and said to the king, "Your lordship, he will not come!" Then the king said, "Tell him that I have no close association with any ascetic. Further, up to now, I have not seen an ascetic. Therefore, please come." Saying so, he sent the minister for the second time.

The ascetic, on hearing this, came to the palace. The king paid him obeisance and asked, "Where do you go, and where do you live?" The ascetic said, "Your lordship, I live in the Himalayan forest. And as it is time to observe the rainy season retreat, I am searching now for a place to live." The king, hearing him, said, "Please live in my pleasure garden." Saying so, he gave him food to eat.

After that, the king led the ascetic to his pleasure garden. He requested the watchman to make arrangements for the ascetic to stay there, and told him to look after the ascetic very carefully. Giving the watchman this responsibility, the king returned to his palace. Since then, the king would go two or three times a day to see the ascetic.

At this time, the king had a son called Wicked [Duṭṭha]. The young prince was very rough and arrogant, and always acted with anger as if he were a snake hit with a stick. He paid no attention to the words of his parents, his relatives, his friends, or others. The king, worried about this

22 Salt and sours are not obtainable in the forest. In ancient times it was believed that these things were necessary to maintain one's bodily health.

situation, took the prince one day to see the ascetic. He said, "Reverend sir, my son is very rough and arrogant. Kindly tame him." Saying so, the king handed over the prince to the ascetic's care, and he went away.

The ascetic became friendly with the prince. Holding his hand while walking in the pleasure garden, he showed him a young neem tree shoot that had only two leaves on it. He said, "Look at this neem tree shoot. Take one of its leaves and taste it." The prince did so, and as the leaf was very bitter, he spit it out with saliva. He then uprooted the young tree with one hand, and said, "If this is bitter like this now, when it becomes a big tree no doubt it will cause unhappiness for many."

The ascetic said, "Look at this. The neem tree was bitter so you uprooted it. In the same way, your father's ministers think of you that you are very rough and arrogant, and that if you become the king no doubt you will do many disastrous things. Thinking so, they too will kill you. Therefore, you must decide not to be rough, arrogant, and bad to people, and must live in a righteous and gentle way." The ascetic advised the prince to be tame in this way.

On hearing this advice, the prince started to lead a life that was not rough and arrogant. After the death of his father, the king, he passed a very righteous and peaceful life and the people of the country prospered. In the end, he passed away leading a righteous life.

"At that time, the wicked prince was the wicked prince of today. The king at that time was the Venerable Ānanda. And the ascetic was I who am today the Buddha who is supreme in the whole world." Saying this, the Buddha ended this Jātaka story.

The moral: "Wise advice can help one change."

150

The Story of Sañjīva
(*Sañjīva-Jātaka*)

When the Buddha was in Jetavanārāma, the king Ajātasattu was friendly with Devadatta. Even though unrighteous and sinful, Ajātasattu was pleased with him. He built for Devadatta a temple in Gayāsīsa, which he gave to him. And he assisted him by giving him all the necessary perquisites. In the meantime, following Devadatta's words, he sent the elephant Nāḷāgiri to kill the Buddha and he sent bowmen to shoot at the Buddha. Many bad things such as these were done by him. After that, his father who was a very righteous king and who was one who had attained the stream entrance state of mind [*sotāpanna*], was killed by him through the persuasion of Devadatta.

Later, he heard that Devadatta had died and had gone to hell sinking down through the earth. On hearing this, he became afraid for his life believing that if anything happened to Devadatta, no doubt it would happen to him, too. He was very much afraid day and night. He spent the daytime in the routine activities of his daily life. But at night, when he went to bed, he dreamed that he was falling through the earth that had opened up and was shooting forth the fires of hell. From this, he became even more afraid as if he were a chicken that had its neck twisted and had been thrown into the hot sun to die. In this way, he suffered day and night despite his royal luxuries.

He had a keen interest in questioning the Buddha about the dream he was having, but he was reluctant to express that interest to Jīvaka. One day he saw the moonlight bright as if it were daylight, and he said to his minister Jīvaka, "The moonlight is so clear that one can see the distance of forty-five arrow shots as if it were daytime. It is not good to waste our time by staying here. This night is pleasant, calm, attractive, and beautiful. Let us go to a good ascetic, to someone like that, to listen to the Dhamma. I have now such an intention. Do you know to whom we can go?" The other ministers who heard him started to mention the names of the various religious masters to whom they each paid obeisance. Most of them were Nigaṇṭha-s. One minister said, "There is the ascetic Pūraṇa Kassapa. He is a Buddha. Let us go to see him." Another minister said, "It would be good to go to the Buddha Makkhali Gosāla." Another minister said, "Instead of going to him, let us go to the Buddha Ajita Keśakambala." Then some other minister wanted to go to the Buddha Kakudha Kaccāyana. After, another said, "I think it would be good to go to the Buddha Sañjaya Belaṭṭhiputta." The sixth one said, "I suggest that more than any other Buddha, Nigaṇṭha Nāthaputta is the best one to whom to go."

In this way, all the ministers said what they thought, mentioning various Nigaṇṭha-s, all of who were like children [with regard to spiritual advancement]. The king did not listen to them seriously, thinking, "No doubt Jīvaka will respond to my question." But Jīvaka was silent. Understanding his silence, the king addressed Jīvaka. He asked, "Jīvaka, these people are all praising their own Buddha-s whom each of them follows. Why do you not say something? Do you have no such a Buddha?"

Jīvaka heard this and got up from his seat. He paid respect toward the direction in which the Buddha was, and he recited the nine-fold virtuousness of the Buddha. He said, "Such a virtuous, omnipresent one is now living in my mango park followed by 1,800 monks. Therefore, I suggest that it would be good for your lordship to go there."

On listening to him, the king said, "It is wonderful. Let us go there." And he made arrangements to go there by elephants together with his retinue. He went to the Buddha in royal magnificence. He approached the Buddha's residence and dismounted his elephant. He then came to the followers of the Buddha who were wearing neat and clean clothes, who had tranquil faculties, who all were seated still with arms and feet close to their bodies, and of whom not even one sneezed or coughed. He was very pleased by seeing this. First he paid his respects to the monks, and then to the Buddha. He sat down and said, "Sir, I would like to ask a question." "Well, your lordship, ask your question." Then the king said, "Venerable sir, what is the result that one can gain by being a monk?" The Buddha said the discourse called the *Sāmaññaphala Sutta* divided into two sections [*bhāṇavāra*-s] and into 500 points to be explained [*grantha*-s].[23]

After this preaching, Ajātasattu knelt down in the presence of the Buddha to pay his respect and said, "Revered sir, please excuse my wrong deeds that I have done out of ignorance." Buddha accepted his apology, and the king went away.

Then the Buddha addressed the monks, saying, "Oh monks, this King Ajātasattu by being associated with a bad person both killed his father and at the same time ruined his chance for future salvation. If he did not do so, he would today be one who has entered into the stream entrance state of mind [*sotāpanna*]."

The next day, the monks assembled in the preaching hall were discussing how King Ajātasattu had lost his good fortune to become a Sotāpanna. The fully enlightened one entered the preaching hall then and asked the monks, "Oh monks, what were you discussing before I came here?" The monks mentioned the previous day's incident. And the Buddha said, "Oh monks, not only in this life but even in the past, Ajātasattu by associating with evil ones created for himself misfortune." The monks invited the Buddha to disclose the past story.

"At one time, when King Brahmadatta was ruling in Benares, the Enlightenment Being was born in a Brahmin family in that city. When he was grown, he went to a well-known teacher who used to teach in the city and began to study under him. After studying under him, he started to teach students on his own.

"While he was teaching students like this, he had a student named Sañjīvaka. He taught him a spell that could be used to bring the dead to

23 The *Sāmaññaphala Sutta* is to be found in the *Dīghanikāya*, but it is not divided there into two sections.

life. And when they gain life, they can walk—but only a short distance. He did not teach him the spell to immobilize them if they come near.

"Once, that student went with a group of other students to fetch firewood from the forest. On their way, they saw a dead tiger on the ground. Sañjīvaka said to the other students, 'Do you want to see my power? I will bring this tiger back to life.' The other students said, 'How can you bring a dead being back to life? It will never happen.' Sañjīvaka said, 'Just look at what I do.' And he started to recite the spell. The other students said, 'Who knows what will happen!' And they climbed up trees.

"While Sañjīvaka was repeating the spell, he threw some pebbles toward the dead body of the tiger. When he was throwing the pebbles, the tiger started to get up. He came forward, and jumping up on the very person who was chanting the spell, he killed him. The tiger that had been brought back to life also fell dead at that spot.

"The other students collected the firewood and returned to where they were studying. They told the teacher what had happened. On hearing the news, the teacher said to the students, "It is not good to help an evil friend. If you do so, such is the result." And he advised them to live generous and peaceful lives. He himself lived such a life, did many meritorious deeds, and acquired much merit. At the end of his life he died, and was born in heaven.

"Sañjīvaka was King Ajātasattu at that time. The teacher of Benares was I who have become the Buddha." In this way, the Buddha ended the story of Sañjīva.

The moral: "Choose your friends wisely."

ABOUT PARIYATTI

Pariyatti is dedicated to providing affordable access to authentic teachings of the Buddha about the Dhamma theory (*pariyatti*) and practice (*paṭipatti*) of Vipassana meditation. A 501(c)(3) non-profit charitable organization since 2002, Pariyatti is sustained by contributions from individuals who appreciate and want to share the incalculable value of the Dhamma teachings. We invite you to visit www.pariyatti.org to learn about our programs, services, and ways to support publishing and other undertakings.

Pariyatti Publishing Imprints

Vipassana Research Publications (focus on Vipassana as taught by S.N. Goenka in the tradition of Sayagyi U Ba Khin)

BPS Pariyatti Editions (selected titles from the Buddhist Publication Society, copublished by Pariyatti)

MPA Pariyatti Editions (selected titles from the Myanmar Pitaka Association, copublished by Pariyatti)

Pariyatti Digital Editions (audio and video titles, including discourses)

Pariyatti Press (classic titles returned to print and inspirational writing by contemporary authors)

Pariyatti enriches the world by

- disseminating the words of the Buddha,
- providing sustenance for the seeker's journey,
- illuminating the meditator's path.

www.ingramcontent.com/pod-product-compliance
Lightning Source LLC
Chambersburg PA
CBHW022132170626
46808CB00002B/956
* 9 7 8 1 6 8 1 7 2 6 5 9 5 *